STEALING
Starlight

DON'T MISS THESE OTHER STAR DARLINGS BOOKS

Sage and the Journey to Wishworld
Libby and the Class Election
Leona's Unlucky Mission
Vega and the Fashion Disaster
Scarlet Discovers True Strength
Cassie Comes Through
Piper's Perfect Dream
Astra's Mixed-Up Mission
Tessa's Lost and Found
Adora Finds a Friend
Clover's Parent Fix
Gemma and the Ultimate Standoff

Good Wish Gone Bad

Wish-a-Day Diary
Wish Cards and Book
A Wisher's Guide to Starland

COMING SOON
Star-Crossed Summer

STEALING
Starlight

Shana Muldoon Zappa and Ahmet Zappa

with Anna Hays

LOS ANGELES • NEW YORK

Printed in the United States of America
First Hardcover Edition, January 2017
FAC-020093-16337
Library of Congress Control Number: 2016951425
ISBN 978-1-4847-5639-3
For more Disney Press fun, visit
www.disneybooks.com

THIS LABEL APPLIES TO TEXT STOCK

Good friends help each
other be great.

Have you ever wondered what happens when you make a wish?

When you blow out your birthday candles, or toss a coin into a fountain, or pull a wishbone apart, your wish goes out into the universe. But what you probably don't know is that your wish turns into a glowing Wish Orb, invisible to the human eye. This orb travels from Earth on a one-way trip to the brightest star in the sky—Starland.

Starland is inhabited by Starlings, who have magical powers that they use to make good wishes come true. When good wishes are granted, the result is positive energy—and Starlings need this energy. It's what keeps their world running. There are different types of wishes:

GOOD WISHES: Positive wishes that come from the heart.

Examples: I wish to get an A in math; I wish I could get along with my sister; I wish to be a fashion designer.

Good Wish Orbs are kept in Wish-Houses. Once the time is right for them to be granted, they begin to sparkle. When that happens the orb is presented to the appropriate Starling, who will travel to find the Wisher and help make it come true.

BAD WISHES: Negative wishes meant for selfish, mean-spirited things.

Examples: I wish my friend would fail; I wish I could control people; I wish my enemy would get hurt.

Bad Wish Orbs are transferred to the Negative Energy Facility. They are very dangerous, filled with negative energy, and must not be granted.

IMPOSSIBLE WISHES: These simply can't be granted by Starlings.

Examples: I wish for world peace; I wish all diseases would disappear; I wish my pet hadn't died.

These extra-bright orbs are contained in a special area of the Wish-House, with the hope that one day they might be turned into good wishes that Starlings can help grant.

INSPIRATIONAL WISHES: Wishes for things that haven't been achieved before.

Examples: I wish to be the first female president; I wish to invent a new vaccine; I wish to be the fastest runner in history.

Massive amounts of positive energy are released when these wishes are granted, but even better, they inspire countless other people to wish for things they thought weren't possible. These wishes show us we shouldn't let ourselves be limited by society's expectations!

Starlings take their wish granting very seriously, especially the twelve Star-Charmed Starlings—the Star Darlings—who attend a special school called Starling Academy. . . .

PROLOGUE

The glimmerdust had finally settled after the standoff between the Star Darlings and the evil Rancora, where they battled over the fate of Starland. Rancora had come incredibly close to turning Starland dark forever with her massive amounts of negative energy. But because the Star Darlings had secretly been visiting Wishworld (known to those who lived there as Earth) and helping grant good wishes, they had collected enough positive energy to overpower Rancora, reverse the damage she had done, and save their world.

What the Star Darlings learned after the

standoff was that Rancora had a troubled history with their beloved mentor, headmistress Lady Stella. The conflict between the two women had begun when they were teens themselves at Starling Academy, many staryears before. And it was clear to the Star Darlings that though Rancora may have been stopped this time, she would be back to seek out her revenge, no matter what it took.

But for now Starland's sky glowed with effervescent purple, fuchsia, and gold stars that danced their way across the horizon. The water surrounding Stellar Falls glistened with tiny silvery sparkles that burst through the rushing surface. All across Starling Academy's campus, featherjabber and druderwomp blooms began to peek out, almost but not quite ready to blossom. The magical display could mean only one thing: the Time of Shadows was ending, making way for a new season. It was just a matter of stardays before the Time of New Beginnings started. . . .

CHAPTER

One

"I'm ready!" Sage said, jumping off the comfy circular swing chair that hung from the ceiling in her room. She adjusted the headband in her wavy lavender hair, smiling as she stared into her dorm room mirror. "Let's do this!"

"Miss Sage, when you put your mind to something, there's no stopping you!" Bot-Bot MO-J4 zoomed around Sage, admiring her determination.

"Thanks, Mojay," Sage said, playfully bowing to him.

Unlike other Bot-Bots, who were simply

guides and helpers to the Starlings at Starling Academy, MO-J4 had taken a special liking to Sage and they'd been friends ever since Sage's first day at the academy. He had been assigned to support all the Star Darlings, but he held a special glow for Sage.

Sage was only a first-year student, but her dream was to become the best Wish-Granter Starland had ever seen. It had always been in Sage's nature to reach way beyond the stars, and she knew the key to being the best Wish-Granter was to gather more positive wish energy than had ever been gathered before.

Even before Sage arrived at the academy, she had set her sights on wish granting and collecting positive wish energy for the good of Starland. Her mother, Indirra, one of the top wish scientists on Starland, was her inspiration. Indirra had raised the bar for any Starling, but it was especially high for her daughter. If Sage had another chance to go down to Wishworld and grant a wish the next day, it wouldn't be soon enough.

Sage adjusted her headband again, then

picked up her star-shaped guitar and started strumming and singing. *"Close your eyes, believe with all your might. Spark a dream, light it up till it turns bright. Nothing in the universe can knock us down . . ."*

MO-J4 buzzed around her. "Shall I bring you a cup of zoomberry tea before I attend to the other Star Darlings?"

Sage stopped singing for a moment. "No need, MO-J4, I'll get it. I need to practice my energy manipulation anyway." She inhaled deeply and squinted. With perfect balance and not a single drop spilled, a cup of steaming zoomberry tea floated across the room and landed safely in Sage's palm.

"Bravo, Miss Sage! You truly are extraordinary."

Sage took a long, satisfying sip and then winked at the Bot-Bot. "Mojay, where would I be without you to cheer me on?"

If it had been possible, MO-J4 would have started humming happily, but since Bot-Bots weren't programmed that way, he replied with a cryptic "Of course, Miss Sage." However, somewhere in his central emotions processing unit, he felt something special for this Starling. He buzzed around Sage's lavender room with the knowledge that he was not only performing the required task of helping the promising first-year Starling, but he was being a friend, too!

While Sage savored her tea, she recalled her first day at the esteemed Starling Academy. How nervous and excited at once she had been! All Starlings, including Sage, arrived with something in common: they had nothing! They came without a single belonging, not even a toothlight. Everything was provided for them. Each Starling's wardrobe was chosen based on her personal taste and style, not to mention her hopes, dreams, and wishes. Courses ranging from Astral Accounting (Sage's least favorite) to Lighterature (Sage's favorite) to Intro to Wish Fulfillment were carefully designed for the lucky Starlings. The girls were admitted to the academy by a select board of leading wish energy experts and top Wish-Granters. The powerful influencers and wise mentors challenged each Starling to explore the most positive side of herself.

It was a secret, though, that among the many gifted Starlings who attended Starling Academy, twelve were part of an ancient prophecy tied to Starland's fate. Their code name was the Star Darlings. Sage's masterful energy manipulation and levitation talents had earned her a spot in this exclusive group of Starlings led by Lady Stella.

MO-J4 zoomed toward the door. He maneuvered around in a perfect circle and beeped, "Anything else, Miss Sage?"

"All good," Sage chirped. She smiled at the cute little flying Bot-Bot. She couldn't resist leaning over to give him a hug, then waved. "Bye, Mojay!"

Unaccustomed to such affection from a Starling, MO-J4 practically short-circuited. "Exiting now, Miss Sage," he replied quickly.

As soon as MO-J4 left, Sage spun around in her swing chair. She concentrated with all the positive wish energy she could conjure. In an instant, she mentally changed the image on her holo-wall from the starry sky in Starland to an electric burst of all her favorite colors: purple, fuchsia, and gold. She sighed. "There! Now for a short nap. Then I can finally catch up on my reading."

Just as she closed her eyes, her Star-Zap pulsated with lavender light. A hologram appeared in front of her. It projected an image of the Star Darlings band onstage at the band shell, setting up for rehearsal. "Band practice!" Sage shrieked. "Starf! I'm late!"

The Star Darlings band had landed a starmazing gig. They were going to play at an event for the upcoming holiday, Light Giving Day. That was the first day of the Time of New Beginnings, when Starlings exchanged glowing gifts with one another. It was only a week away, and they still hadn't come up with a song for the festivities.

Sage heard a light tap at the door. It was MO-J4. He had returned to remind Sage about band rehearsal, albeit a bit late. He zoomed into Sage's room in a great rush, trying to make up for his momentary memory blip. He insisted, "You must be mindful of the time. You've got practice with the Star Darlings band in five starmins. Shall I pack up your guitar?"

Sage said hurriedly, "I'm already on it, Mojay!" She put her energy manipulation skills to work once again, this time sending her sparkling guitar inside its case and snapping it shut with great precision. "Yes!"

Her hidden dresser drawers popped up from the sunken floor, and with a swipe of her hand, out floated the most perfect outfit for just that kind of day—a day of sparkling starshine, new beginnings, and sweet music.

MO-J4 cleared the way for Sage as she raced down the Little Dipper Dorm hallways, out to the Star Quad, and toward the band shell. Sage opted to fly to the band shell instead of jumping on the Cosmic Transporter. She was in a hurry, after all, and she had the energy manipulation skills needed for it! Hovering above the busy Starling Academy campus, she blurred past the other Starlings, leaving a sparkling lavender-scented trail behind her. She sped past Lady Stella, who turned and smiled at her star student.

"Star greetings, Sage," Lady Stella said softly.

Sage waved to the headmistress as she continued on her way to the band shell. "Star greetings, Lady Stella. Gotta jam now!"

She hoped she would get to practice before the rest of the band had finished tuning up. As she neared her destination, Sage thought about how, in just a few starmins, she'd be playing music with the Star Darlings band. She brightened, knowing that music always brought her comfort, sort of like sipping zoomberry tea or relaxing on the giant soft sofa in her parents' house. Then she picked up speed and whizzed past a glimmerwillow tree.

CHAPTER

Two

"La, la, la, la, la!" Leona warmed up her voice, stretching her mouth in all sorts of crazy shapes. She had always dreamed of being a lead singer, and now there she was in the Star Darlings band! *"La-la-la-la-la-la-la. Me-me-me-me-me-me!"*

Scarlet, the drummer in the band, smirked. "Singing about you-you-you-you-you-you again, Leona?"

Leona gave her a look, annoyed. She and the ultra-sarcastic Scarlet had very different personalities, to say the least. "Warming up, Scarlet. . . . *Me-me-me-me-me.*" Leona counted her lucky stars every time she had the chance to stand in front of a microphone and sing for an audience. She wasn't going to let one of Scarlet's *moods* get in the way of her enjoying herself. Leona's one big personal rule as a singer was never to sing without first warming up her voice. After all, her voice was her instrument and it needed to be treated with great care. *"La-tee, la-tee, la-tee, tah!"* Then she stopped herself. "What's your secret to warming up, Scarlet?"

"It wouldn't be a secret if I told you, now, would it?" Scarlet retorted as she adjusted her drum kit, tightening the cymbals.

Leona shook off Scarlet's snarky remark. Scarlet was just being Scarlet. Leona knew her all too well, since they had been roommates from day one at the academy. Leona did sometimes think that if Scarlet would open up even just a little bit to the other Star Darlings, maybe she would smile more.

Scarlet rolled her eyes and let her attention drift to the music she was listening to on her headphones. She picked up her shimmering fuchsia drumsticks and tried out a particularly difficult rhythm, but the beat escaped her. She just couldn't get it right.

Vega stood near the corner of the stage, methodically tuning her bass guitar with her brand-new Star-Zap holo-tuner. Finally, the tuner glowed an intense blue that matched the deep color of her bass. She pumped her fists in the air. "Awesomeness!" She turned to Leona and nodded. "I'm good over here. My new holo-tuner was seriously the most startastic purchase I have ever made. I swear I don't know how I ever played without it."

Libby smiled. "Sweet, Vega!" She strapped on her keytar and warmed up her fingers on the keyboard. She grinned at the thought that the Ranker had actually chosen her to be in the Star Darlings band. She still couldn't believe it. Libby was so pleased that all those years of classical piano lessons had led to her being in the stellar band. It made every awkward recital totally worth it.

Sage arrived, out of breath, and slipped onstage, unnoticed by the four other members of the band.

"Made it!" she whispered to herself, and used her energy manipulation to quickly tune her guitar. Then, pretending she wasn't out of breath, she grabbed a microphone to check the sound levels on her mic stand. "Asteroid, asteroid, sparklebright, sparklebright, asteroid!"

Scarlet adjusted her seat at the drums and twirled her trusty glowing drumsticks. She tapped out a few familiar rhythms, then again attempted the drum trick she had tried earlier, but she still couldn't get it right. Frustrated, she stopped playing altogether. Scarlet couldn't figure out why she was having so much trouble with that particular drum trick; she had thought it would be easy. Her mind-body-drumstick coordination must be off-balance. She reminded herself to focus and not let anything distract her. She tried the drum rhythm again, infusing a blast of energy manipulation that time, but for some reason, it still wasn't coming together.

Leona noticed Scarlet struggling on the drums. Now it was her turn to tease Scarlet. "You're not dreaming about living on Wishworld again, are you?"

Scarlet lowered her head and didn't say a word. She pulled her sparkling velvet hoodie over her pink-and-black-streaked bob, covering her eyes, and leaned back to wait for rehearsal to begin for real.

Maybe Leona was right. Scarlet couldn't remember a time when she hadn't thought about what it would be like to live on Wishworld. She even called it Earth, just like the Wishlings who lived there did. In the privacy of her dorm room, when she retreated to her private reading nook, she would often holo-project images from various locales on Wishworld. Sometimes they would be snowcapped mountaintops or deep blue oceans. Other times she would visualize busy city streets or miles and miles of green countryside. She had a restless feeling inside her that she just couldn't explain, but she was convinced that it had to do with her belonging on Wishworld.

Scarlet knew if given the chance, down on Wishworld, she could press the refresh button, so to speak, and her inner light would shine as brightly as the sun. She could be more herself there—not like on Starland, where she felt like an outsider. Lately, she'd been longing to escape there and finding it more difficult than ever to hide her feeling that she just didn't fit in with the rest of the Starlings.

All tuned up now, Sage called out to the others, "Ready to rock this thing?" Everyone nodded. She switched her Star-Zap to record mode for the session.

"Here's something I've been working on for the last few stardays," she went on. "Join in whenever you like. Maybe we can spin it into the song for our Light Giving Day gig. . . ." Sage began strumming the first few chords on her guitar.

Libby added a musical layer to the song on her keytar. "How's this?"

Sage moved to the beat. "Yes, Libby! Love it!"

Vega followed with a solid bass line, while Scarlet found a steady beat on the drums. Leona hummed along, throwing in some fun improvised lyrics here and there. They played for a few starmins, then Sage signaled her bandmates to stop. "This is sounding great!" she said. "And

I don't want to rush anyone's creative process, but I think we have to get down to the business of actually writing a song." Sage's eyes widened. "Everyone at the academy will be at Light Giving Day, including Lady Stella. We're going to totally crush it, I know it. We just need to come up with the right sound and lyrics for the occasion," she added with a tinge of nerves and excitement. "Any ideas?"

Leona spoke up. "As long as it's in my key, we'll soar higher than the moon! Lady Stella will love it!"

Vega, who was one of the more serious girls in the group, tried to illuminate the others. "We all know that Light Giving Day is about celebrating a new season. Why don't we create a song about the seasonal changes at the Time of New Beginnings, like the first blooms of the druderwomps and featherjabbers?"

Libby giggled animatedly. "Don't forget that it's also about exchanging gifts. And gift-giving is one of my all-time favorite things to do in the galaxy! Any time of the staryear or any season.

For sure, we should write about that. You know, how it feels when you give someone the perfect present!"

"Although we do exchange gifts," Vega added, "technically speaking, Light Giving Day is really about the cosmological alignment of all the gleaming stars on Starland linking together to produce an electric array of pure positive energy, the purest of any starlight on Starland." Vega enjoyed sharing her stellar knowledge of starology whenever she saw the opportunity. Band practice on this starry afternoon was no exception.

"Highly informative, Vega," Scarlet said sarcastically as she tapped her drums, testing the pitch.

Sage's Star-Zap blinked madly, overloaded from recording the Star Darlings' flood of creative suggestions.

"Whatever we decide," Leona insisted, "the lyrics have to flow so my voice will stand out. If I don't feel it, it's just not going to glow."

Sage sighed, taking into account all her friends' input. "Let's see what we've got so far." She looked down at her Star-Zap. Suddenly, it flickered. All the ideas and music that she'd been recording during rehearsal disappeared into nothingness. "Oh, no! There must be some kind of glitch!"

She quickly turned to Leona. "Hey, can I borrow your Star-Zap? I've got to holo-text Mojay for techno help!"

"My stars, yes!" Leona quickly handed Sage her golden glitter-covered Star-Zap, and Sage holo-texted her favorite Bot-Bot.

Scarlet was unaware that the entire collaborative songwriting session had just vaporized. Continuing to tap at her drums, she found a backbeat she liked for the song. "How's this?" she asked.

"Oh, yeah, Scarlet. Nice!" Leona began to sing a random assortment of lyrics that came into her head. Then she pretended she was receiving an award in front of hydrongs of Starlings. "Really? A contract to sing for *Voices of the Stars*? Me?"

The Star Darlings giggled at Leona's antics.

Scarlet smirked. "Really, Leona? That's all you could come up with for the new song?"

Vega and Libby played along and attempted

to add to the musical experiment, but soon it was clear that the song was woefully off-key and seriously not coming together on all accounts.

"Rehearsal is officially over due to, uh, a technical glitch!" Sage announced, handing Leona back her Star-Zap. She had just learned that MO-J4 was in the Bot-shop getting his wires checked, so he wouldn't be around to help with her much-needed Star-Zap until the following morning. She was Star-Zapless for the time being, and the band wasn't even close to creating a new song for Light Giving Day. For the first time since Lady Stella had offered the Star Darlings center stage at the celebration, Sage wondered if writing a new song with the Star Darlings band was going to be as easy as she had imagined.

CHAPTER
Three

Alone, far above the band shell, Vivica studied
the Star Darlings' practice from behind a glorange
blossom tree. She had long straight silvery-blue
hair with bangs, and steely blue eyes, which were
currently fixed on Leona. As Vivica watched
from afar, she stung with jealousy as she imagined the Star Darlings band playing effortlessly,
shining brighter than all the other Starlings at
the academy. As she fumed, she pursed her lips
and muttered angrily, "Star Dippers!"

It seemed like only a starmin ago that Vivica
had been just another naive student at Starling
Academy. Talented and beautiful, yet fiercely

competitive, Vivica craved popularity and longed to be included in the Star Darlings' inner circle. Though, at the time, she hadn't known they were called the Star Darlings. She only knew they were a special group she had been excluded from. When she first learned of their special class at the end of each day, she sensed that there was more to the story. And, as she paid more attention, it seemed unlikely that these twelve Starlings needed additional help with their studies. They were some of the most powerful and talented girls in school. She poked fun at their group name, calling them "Star Dippers," but she was really trying to uncover the true purpose of those secret classes.

Now that Vivica knew the truth—that the Star Darlings were handpicked by Lady Stella and sent on secret Wish Missions to collect positive wish energy for Starland—everything had changed. Vivica's throat tightened. A chill ran down her spine every time she thought about being left out from this select group of Starlings. She could not understand why she hadn't been chosen to be a Star Darling. She felt sure her wish granting and wish energy manipulation skills were just as advanced as any of those girls'.

Vivica was intently watching the Star Darlings band rehearse when, suddenly, something startled her. She turned to see what it was, but saw nothing there. She felt something, though. A cool breeze circled her, giving her the chills. As the breeze increased in strength, a handful of glorange blossom leaves fluttered around her.

"What's going on?" Vivica whispered softly. She looked around, not sure what she was searching for. Then she spotted a necklace, floating through the air as if carried by the wind. It was made of a thin dark rope, with a pendant shaped like a droplet. It was the most unique and lovely necklace that she'd ever seen. Vivica reached for it and began to examine it more closely. The pendant felt heavy and seemed important somehow. It swirled with beautiful dark hues of purple and black. She looked around to make sure nobody was watching and moved to put it on, but then she heard a voice.

"Here, let me help you with that," a woman said. "There's a trick to tightening the clasp."

Vivica quickly looked up. There, standing before her, was Rancora, Starland's fiercest enemy. She was the Starling who had tried to destroy Starland by draining it of all positive energy. Rancora was a terrifying figure, with her sharp angled features and piercing eyes that blazed with anger. Vivica stepped back, inhaling sharply.

Rancora tried to reassure Vivica. "Relax, my sparkling Starling. No need to be frightened."

Vivica froze in her tracks. The last thing she wanted to do was upset Rancora. Vivica clutched the necklace in her hand. "You're not supposed to be . . ."

"Here? On Starland?" Rancora smiled. "Do you really think Lady Stella could stop me from my destiny?" She caught herself as she started to raise her voice. It certainly wasn't her intention to scare Vivica. Quite the opposite, actually. She needed Vivica's trust. She had plans for the young girl. Softening her tone, she reached out her hand for the necklace, which Vivica willingly gave her. With the other hand, Rancora lifted her finger to her lips. "Hush and listen, my Starling."

Vivica stood perfectly still. The breeze that had been stirring was now calm, and the silence in the air made Vivica uneasy. *What does Rancora want from me? And why is she here on Starland?*

Rancora held the necklace high against the starry sky. Its surface was like a dark iridescent mirror. Vivica was entranced by it.

Rancora studied Vivica as she admired the teardrop necklace. "Vivica, you know that I was just like you when I was a student here at the academy, many years ago. Beautiful, young, and talented. Then it happened. *She* happened!" Rancora trembled. "Lady Stella betrayed me so she could climb her way up the constellations. And I was left with . . . nothing!"

Vivica watched Rancora swing the necklace back and forth in front of her eyes, following it as it swung from left to right.

"Now I have an opportunity for you. I think you're the perfect Starling. I'd like you to go on a Wish Mission for me."

"A Wish Mission?" Vivica asked, her eyes still transfixed on the swinging necklace.

"Yes! You see, just before I found you here, I was able to sneak into Starling Academy without Lady Stella or her *impeccable* staff or any Bot-Bots taking notice. Fueled by the remaining droozle of negatites I had left in this pendant, I landed undetected. My timing couldn't have been more perfect, for just as my heels touched Starland, a Bad Wish Orb flew overhead on its way to the Negative Energy Facility. I intercepted it, steadied it, and then went inside the orb to learn the nature of the wish burning inside."

Vivica listened with great anticipation. She was entranced. "And what did you see?"

"A glimpse into a wonderful negative wish on Wishworld, of course!"

"Oh, how interesting!" Vivica exclaimed.

"It was indeed. You will see in time, the more missions you embark on, the more thrilling each one becomes."

Vivica listened, fully captivated by Rancora. "What happens next is all part of my plan for you, my Starling," Rancora promised.

Vivica smiled broadly, feeling more comfortable around Rancora now. "You have a plan for *me*?"

Rancora rolled the teardrop pendant between her palms lovingly. "What I saw inside the Bad Wish Orb was a young girl who stood just outside the doors of a theater. She appeared to be very upset about something."

Rancora began to cough. Her hands shook. Vivica watched, concerned, as Rancora physically weakened before her eyes. "Are you feeling okay, Rancora?" she asked.

Unwilling to admit her weakness, Rancora snapped, "I'm fine." Then, catching herself losing her temper, she softened again. "You see, I learned that our Wisher's name is Clara, and she's a singer. She wants to step out of the shadows and be center stage. She is sick of her best friend, Holly, stealing the starlight." Rancora paused, looking into Vivica's eyes.

"Does this feeling of living in the shadows mean anything to you, Vivica?" she asked pointedly.

Vivica's body instantly tensed and she replied,

"Of course, it does! I wonder every day, why wasn't *I* chosen to be a Star Darling? Why wasn't *I* picked to lead the Star Darlings band? Why have I been overlooked here on Starland time and time again, when I am just as talented as Leona or any of the other Star Darlings?"

Vivica paused as the teardrop necklace crackled.

"Are you asking me to help grant this wish?" she asked Rancora. Vivica had dreamed of taking the shooting star journey to Wishworld. So far, the twelve Star Darlings at Starling Academy had been the only students who were allowed to travel to Wishworld. And here was an opportunity for her to grant a Wisher's wish, just like the Star Darlings had done under the watchful eye of Lady Stella.

"Yes, my Starling. And you will be greatly rewarded." Rancora lifted the teardrop necklace and clasped it around Vivica's neck. A jolt of negative energy coursed through Vivica's body. The necklace crackled again. Vivica jumped back, surprised by the new feeling inside her.

She touched the finely shaped teardrop, and a wicked smile appeared on her face. "I've never received an important gift like this before, not from anyone." She shivered with excitement. She couldn't believe her good fortune.

Rancora caught her breath, then spoke in a hushed tone, playing on Vivica's insecurities. "Vivica, time to wake up and smell the Zing. The Star Darlings, under Lady Stella's guidance, are stealing *your* starlight. As long as Lady Stella serves as headmistress," she hissed, *"you will never shine!"* Rancora started to cough again. This time her cough was more intense. Her energy was visibly fading. She needed to retreat back to the Isle of Misera, but she knew that this angry young Starling was her way to control the balance of energy on Starland. She needed to recruit Vivica to her side. And now that Vivica was being infused with negative energy from the teardrop pendant around her neck, the girl would be happy to help her.

Vivica looked around, checking to see if anyone else was nearby. Her heart beat faster with each thought that raced through her mind. She couldn't tell if she was afraid or thrilled. Perhaps it was a little of both. "I'll do it! I'll help grant the bad wish on Wishworld!" she blurted out.

Rancora took a deep breath. "Lovely. Time for me to retreat. More rest is needed for me to regain my strength, but mostly what I need is more negative wish energy." She paused. "That's why your mission is so urgent. I must return now to the Isle of Misera." She stared into Vivica's eyes. "Store all the negative energy you collect from the bad wish in this teardrop pendant and bring the necklace back to me as soon as it has been granted. It will help restore me back to full power. If you can do that, I will make you my one and only apprentice! A shooting star will be waiting to take you to Wishworld this evening."

As Rancora had guessed she would be, Vivica was eager to grant the wish and prove that she was as capable as any Star Darling! She was excited to become Rancora's apprentice.

She had played right into Rancora's plan. Of course, Rancora had a plan! She always did. She had found the third part of an ancient oracle that foretold the fate of Starland, and it involved Vivica.

But what about the first two parts of the oracle? The first one had been discovered years ago, and told of Rancora's—then Cora's—unlawful trip to Starland, the one that caused negative energy to be released on Starland for the first time ever. The second part of the oracle had been discovered by Lady Stella, and it prophesied that twelve Star-Charmed Starlings would save Starland from a massive energy crisis. It was how Lady Stella had come to select the Star Darlings, who would defeat Rancora in her plot to turn Starland dark. But the third part of the oracle . . . Oh, that was the part Stella knew nothing about! The thought of it made Rancora tremble with delight. *She*, not Stella, had discovered that piece, and it was perhaps the most important part! And what it said, well, that was where Vivica came in. The third part of the oracle prophesied that a dark Starling would determine the ultimate fate of Starland. And Rancora knew that dark Starling was young

Vivica. If Rancora could control her, that meant she would control the fate of *all of Starland*! It was everything she had ever wanted.

In a flash, Rancora disappeared, right in front of Vivica's eyes. She left a burning, sour scent in her wake. For a moment, Vivica's eyes stung. A cool breeze washed over her, but this time it didn't give her chills. She touched the teardrop necklace, just to make sure this opportunity of a Cycle of Life wasn't merely a dream.

Before she had time to fully register what was happening, she felt a powerful new surge of negativity overtake her. Even the small amount of negative energy contained inside the necklace had begun to work. Vivica found herself over-whelmed with a sense of clarity and purpose, with a darker heart filled with envy and revenge.

Vivica turned back to the band shell, where the Star Darlings had been practicing, but they were gone. She wondered just how long she'd been standing there under the glorange blossom tree with the forbidden visitor.

Vivica knew that she could not waste even

one starmin in preparing for her Wish Mission. She headed straight to her Little Dipper Dorm room to collect her things . . . then she would journey down to Wishworld on her very first Wish Mission!

CHAPTER

Four

"Ohm. Light the stars. Clear the way," Lady Stella chanted. She inhaled deeply, then bowed and exhaled. The headmistress of Starling Academy sat in the Serenity Gardens, deep in meditation. She whispered in a calm tone, "Salutations to the stars." Lifting her head with her eyes still closed, she inhaled and exhaled once more before opening her eyes again. She looked around the hidden peaceful surroundings she had first discovered when she was a student at the academy. She retreated there whenever she needed time on her own to reflect. Lady Stella was well-known as one of the most powerful Wish-Granters on

Starland, but Rancora's plot to drain Starland of positive energy had thrown her for a loop. She knew that calm inner reflection was important for her to be at her best, so she had been coming to the gardens a lot recently to ponder Starland's future.

Even though the Star Darlings had collected enough positive energy to stop Rancora in her attempt to turn Starland dark, Lady Stella knew that more must be done to protect Starland from this worthy enemy. She could tell from the flutter in her heart that even though Rancora was weakened in body, in spirit she was as determined as ever to see Starland destroyed, taken over with negative energy.

Lady Stella's Star-Zap flashed with a new message from Professor Eugenia Bright about a Starling who had not reported to Wish Fulfillment class, and she realized it was time to get back to her office. She saw a blast of Star-Zap messages she had missed while she had been meditating, and she wanted to review them so she could finish academy business for the day. She stood up and stretched her arms toward the sky. There was something about the stillness of the air that early evening that invited her to take the more scenic route back to her office, through the orchard and past the Celestial Café. On that particular evening, the stars shone extra bright.

As Lady Stella strolled through campus, the Wishworld Surveillance Deck was just ahead of her. *What a perfect night to take a glimpse of Wishworld and see how our Wishling friends are faring,* she thought. *I'll stop for only a moment, then get back to work.*

Her long, flowing white skirt shimmered in the evening light as she ascended the stairs to the Wishworld Surveillance Deck to enjoy the colorful sky and see what she might observe on Wishworld. Those who had ever spent even a starmin at the academy knew that from up high on the deck, you were granted the most glorious view on all of Starland.

Lady Stella looked out on the deck. She breathed in the crisp, clear evening air. The moment she closed her eyes, a rush of thoughts from the recent revelation about Rancora's deception took over. She reflected back to when Rancora was still just *Cora*, a young Starling student at the academy many staryears ago. Lady Stella caught herself speaking aloud. "What has happened to you, Cora? Will you ever find your way back to yourself again?"

Lady Stella visualized the innocent Cora, a young, smart, giggly girl. Cora had been Lady Stella's best friend and roommate while they both attended Starling Academy. That was before their secret trip to Wishworld—before they were caught by their own headmistress and before Cora was expelled. Lady Stella's reflections took her back to the time when she and Cora had first met at the Little Dipper Dorm. What fun they had shared, dancing to tunes on their star player and eating starlight snacks, like moonberry crumbles and cocomoon delights, their absolute favorites. Once friends, now they were enemies.

Lady Stella sighed. How she wished things had gone differently.

That fateful day, when Cora was exposed to the negatites in the Negative Energy Facility and began her transformation into Rancora,

Lady Stella had lost her best friend. Now time had passed and she and Rancora stood on opposite sides of a powerful and dangerous struggle between positive wish energy and negative wish energy. The very fate of Starland hung in the balance.

Something shook Lady Stella from her reflective state. It was a cool wind that tickled her nose. She opened her eyes once again, looking out to the swirling lights in the sky for a clue as she pondered Starland's fragile future. Her eyes opened just in time to witness a streak of colors in the sky that she had never seen before. A shooting star sparked and sputtered, then fell in an unfamiliar zigzag pattern toward Wishworld. Instead of the usual formation of rainbow trails, glowing with soft light and color, this star torpedoed toward Wishworld, leaving a spiky black and steely blue trail.

Lady Stella was taken aback. It almost looked as if—no, it couldn't be. *Is that a Starling traveling down to Wishworld?* For a moment, she convinced herself otherwise. That was impossible.

Yet the colors and the movements . . . There was something just not right about that shooting star, not right at all.

The sky suddenly went completely black. A crackle accompanied by a flicker of lights shot across the sky. Then it began to rain, which was quite out of the ordinary. Not a sparkle shower, either, but tiny spiky hail. Small shards of frozen ice fell furiously from the sky. Lady Stella stepped back, still refusing to believe what she was seeing as she watched the hail disrupt the once tranquil sky.

She knew in her heart that she must act, and act quickly. She managed to make her way back across the Star Quad to her office, drenched and shivering from the cold ice. As soon as she entered her office, the storm calmed, almost as if by command. Lady Stella looked out her window and noticed something unusual outside. The Starling Academy campus was completely dry. She rushed down the hallway and stepped back outside, then leaned down to touch the ground. There wasn't a drop of moisture anywhere.

A flash of light shot through the sky toward the Isle of Misera. Lady Stella studied the star trail closely. The ominous purple and black light that sparked and crackled before fading held great interest for her. She steadied herself and exclaimed with great certainty, "It's her! Rancora has been here!"

CHAPTER

Five

Leona twirled around, singing at the top of her lungs, *"La me, la me, la meeeee!"*

Scarlet was setting up her drums for rehearsal. "How about we start with the melody first this time, Leona?" She smirked.

Leona scrunched up her nose and waved impishly at Scarlet. "Just testing out my vocal range, Scar."

Sage had called a last-minute evening practice session at the Lightning Lounge. She was determined to find inspiration for the song the Star Darlings band had signed up to perform for Light Giving Day. They still needed to write a song for the celebration, and Sage was feeling the time pressure. She ran through a series of chords on her guitar while the others prepped their instruments, hoping the band could come together to create just the right song.

Leona continued her vocal warm-ups, creating even stranger sounds this time around. Scarlet shook her head, then put on her headphones to block out the noise. Suddenly, the light in the sky flickered out long enough to distract Sage from her chord progressions.

Leona stopped warming up. "Uh, anyone just see that?" she asked nervously.

"Must be the atmospheric changes that occur this time of year," Vega stated matter-of-factly. "It's very rare, along the lines of the total eclipse of a purple moon. Statistically, this sort of celestial event can happen just before the Time of New Beginnings."

Through the window, the Star Darlings saw the light in the sky flicker out again. This time the blackness lasted longer.

Vega blinked a few times, then looked up at the sky, searching for another logical explanation for what was happening. Before any of the other Star Darlings could offer their thoughts on the mysterious flickering light, their Star-Zaps flashed with matching messages that read: URGENT! PLEASE COME TO MY OFFICE AT ONCE!

Lady Stella had called an emergency meeting of the Star Darlings. It was most unusual for that time of night.

Scarlet saw the message from Lady Stella on her Star-Zap. She turned down the music she was listening to and took out her earbuds.

Leona dramatically covered her mouth with her hands and gasped in her typical theatrical fashion. "What could this possibly mean?"

"Any Starling knows that there's something out of tune when the Starland sky light flickers," Scarlet said, breaking down her drum set.

Sage wondered if positive wish energy could be draining, since flickering lights had been the first sign of negatites affecting the balance of energy on Starland. "This starlight display is more than just a celestial event. . . . Starland is in trouble," she announced to her bandmates.

The Star Darlings agreed. They hurriedly

packed up their instruments and headed straight to Lady Stella's office, without another note played or a single word spoken.

At the meeting in her office, Lady Stella paced the sparkling floor with an intensity that alarmed all twelve Star Darlings. They sat at her round table, waiting to hear what news she would share with them. They knew better than to say anything or even ask questions. The deafening silence in the room made it crystal clear that something of great importance was happening.

Lady Stella began to speak with urgency in her voice. "My young Starlings. Much has transpired on Starland. We have faced many dangers and overcome them all. I have all of you to thank for that. Now we find ourselves facing a new challenge. Does any Starling know why we're all here this evening?"

Sage offered her explanation. "Could it have something to do with the light flickering in the sky?"

"Yes, Sage, but there's more. My discovery

of the long-forgotten ancient oracle that foretold of twelve Starlings who held the secret to saving Starland was just the beginning of the puzzle. Now I believe there is much more to uncover, and I'll need your help."

"What's happened this time, Lady Stella?" Leona asked nervously. "What can we do?"

"Sh-should we be concerned?" Libby stuttered. "I don't understand."

Lady Stella took a long deliberate sip from her oversized mug of warm Zing. "Our last encounter with Rancora was a test for us all. And we succeeded. However, there were mistakes made. Mistakes that have led to this moment." She took another sip of Zing and announced, "Starland is once again in danger!"

The Star Darlings froze in their seats. Sage closed her eyes, bracing for the worst.

"I've learned that Rancora has intercepted a Bad Wish Orb," Lady Stella continued.

"I can't hear this!" Leona leaped out of her seat.

Scarlet leaned over to calm her down. "Sit down, Leona. Now is not the time to lose it."

Leona's excitable nature didn't serve any Star Darling at that moment. The best thing the Star Darlings could do was remain calm and listen to what Lady Stella had to say.

Sage reassured Leona and the others. "We're going to deal with whatever comes our way."

"We're Star Darlings!" Clover added.

Lady Stella resumed pacing around her office. "Now, where was I . . . Ah, yes. It's not clear how much negative energy Rancora has left, now that I've drained the reserve she was storing on the Isle of Misera. But I know it isn't very much. However, I believe it was enough to have affected a student here at Starling Academy. Somehow, this particular student's memory did not get erased after we defeated Rancora. She knows everything about the Star Darlings and about our Wish Missions to Wishworld. I believe this Starling is now under Rancora's control."

Lady Stella found it difficult to hide her concern and frustration about the difficult situation. She turned away from the Star Darlings to compose herself. When she turned back, she spoke.

"Just moments ago, I saw an unusual colored streak of light shoot through the sky. I am convinced it was Vivica, heading to Wishworld to grant a bad wish for a Wisher."

"Vivica?" Sage blurted out.

"Of course, it's Vivica!" Piper exclaimed.

"Who else would it be?" Scarlet added. She shook her head in disappointment.

Lady Stella continued. "First Professor Eugenia Bright reported Vivica absent this morning from Wish Fulfillment class, and when I checked my messages, I saw that Vivica had not attended Professor Margaret Dumarre's Wishling Ways class, either. When I tried to contact her, she didn't answer. Several Bot-Bots searched everywhere for her, but she couldn't be found. That's when all the crystals fell into place. Rancora must have found a vulnerable Starling in Vivica, who for one reason or another was more susceptible to negative influences than the rest of you, and exposed her to negative energy."

The Star Darlings looked at one another knowingly.

"Yep, that sounds like Vivica," Scarlet sighed.

"She is negative, but would she really go that far?" Adora wondered.

Lady Stella continued. "The level of exposure Vivica had is still unknown. But the negative energy will enhance Vivica's worst instincts. Her better self has been overpowered by Rancora's dark forces. As we sit here on Starland, Vivica is on her way to Wishworld to grant a Wisher a bad wish. If granted, this bad wish will most likely produce enough negative wish energy to restore Rancora's negative power. Since Vivica is a young Wish-Granter, and the Wisher is young, too, the power will be that much greater—as you know."

Lady Stella took a deep breath and another long sip from her cup of Zing in an attempt to calm herself. "For this journey, a Wish Orb will not simply choose a Star Darling to go to Wishworld. It is more complex than that this time. This is a dire situation, not only because if the bad wish is granted, it will give Rancora the negative energy she needs to gain strength . . .

but it will also have a terrible permanent negative affect on Vivica."

The Star Darlings looked anxiously around the room, each wondering who would be chosen to stop the bad wish from being granted by one of their own.

Lady Stella cleared her throat. "I've managed to learn that the Wisher is named Clara and she's a student in a performing arts program at a place called the North Coast Performing Arts Center. I believe Clara's wish is something that will hurt her best friend in some way. I don't know any more beyond that."

The Star Darlings listened quietly to Lady Stella's every word.

"Since the potential threat to Starland's positive energy is so extreme, one Star Darling will not suffice. Nor will two. There must be three Star Darlings sent to Wishworld to stop Vivica before she grants Clara's bad wish."

Lady Stella paused, and a glowing Wish Orb appeared. It hovered around the room, first drifting over to Scarlet. It glowed with the rich fuchsia color of Scarlet's ravenstone Power Crystal. Scarlet blushed almost the same fuchsia color as it floated in front of her. She stared at the glowing orb and then looked at Lady Stella. "I've got this!" Scarlet said. Images of Wishworld flashed before her. She was grateful to have another opportunity to visit Wishworld, even if the journey would test her strength and resilience more than ever. Scarlet knew she was ready.

Lady Stella nodded in silence.

The floating, glowing orb then made its way to the next Star Darling who would take the challenging journey to Wishworld. It was Leona!

Leona yelped, astonished and flattered that she had been chosen. "Lady Stella, I'm honored beyond words." She bowed her head to Lady Stella.

Lady Stella bowed back to her.

As for the third Star Darling who would take the journey, the glowing orb finally landed in front of Sage. She froze in her seat. It was what she had been wishing for, and now there it was!

"Thank you for the honor, Lady Stella. I won't let you down," Sage promised.

"I have great faith in you, Sage."

Sage was thrilled, maybe even more than the others, to be taking such an important journey, because each successful mission brought her closer to her goal. The other Star Darlings gathered around Sage, Leona, and Scarlet. They congratulated the chosen Starlings, offering their help in any way they could provide it.

"We must hurry now. Time to prepare," Lady Stella said, dismissing the Star Darlings.

Sage was the last of the girls to leave. Lady Stella stopped her at the door and motioned for her to return to the office. "Sage, I'd like to talk with you. Please come in and sit down."

Sage wondered why she had been singled out. Had she said something to upset Lady Stella? She found a seat at the round table.

Lady Stella joined her. "Sage," she said with great seriousness and sincerity, "I know that I've given you a challenge beyond what I could have ever imagined taking on when I was a student at the academy."

"Thank you, Lady Stella. I'll do my best to stop the bad wish from being granted."

"Your mother has an extraordinary legacy. She continues to make great advances in wish science for Starland. However, in you, my young Starling, there are untapped gifts that are yours alone, gifts that even you are not wholly aware of yet. You have the power to be a great leader, and I am counting on you to bring that to this journey. Remember that while you are on Wishworld. Now off you go. There's very little time to prepare, so hurry, my dear, hurry!"

CHAPTER

Six

"You are a star. Light up the world!" Leona recited in the mirror. She glowed with anticipation for her latest mission to Wishworld. Her room was a blur of rainbow colors and shimmering lights. She didn't even notice the encouraging message from Lady Stella that flashed on her Star-Zap: LEONA, MY STARLING. YOU ARE READY FOR THIS. REMEMBER, THIS MISSION IS BIGGER THAN ANY ONE STARLING. IT'S FOR ALL OF STARLAND! PREPARE WISELY.

Leona was traveling to Wishworld again! *Oh, my stars. Another chance to make an impression on Wishworld and on Lady Stella,* she thought.

She grabbed a microphone from her dorm room stage and started singing her Mirror Mantra this time. *"You are a star. Light up the world!"* She felt a surge of positive energy rush through her. She twirled around her room and pushed through her starlight curtains, gently falling backward onto her silky golden-covered platform bed that was sprinkled with oversized soft pillows. She grabbed a pillow and squeezed it tightly with excitement. "No broken Wish Pendants this time, Leona. You're going to prove that you are up for the challenge!"

She thought about the moment when Lady Stella had presented her glisten paw Power Crystal to her. The crystal held great cosmic power that she hoped would help her through this uncharted mission.

Leona quickly went through the Wishworld Outfit Selector on her Star-Zap. She knew she would have to blend in with the Wishlings, meaning no obvious sparkle or shine, no glistening skin or brightly colored hair. But who said that "blending in" meant you had to be dull?

Leona was convinced she could still make a fashion statement without exposing the precious secret that she was actually a Starling on a time-sensitive mission to save her home star.

It's time for some star power! Scarlet's Mirror Mantra ran through her mind as she contemplated her next mission. She soared on her skateboard, catching air on her dorm room skate ramp and landing an ollie kickflip. "Nailed it!" she exclaimed, psyching herself up to go back to Wishworld. She grabbed her skateboard and took a break to step in front of her mirror. She recited her Mirror Mantra aloud for extra positive energy. "It's time for some star power!" Scarlet couldn't help smiling at her reflection. "I'm going to Wishworld. This is better than awesome!" she exclaimed excitedly.

After taking a refreshing sparkle shower, followed by rigorous brushing with her toothlight, Scarlet reminded herself that on Wishworld, Wishlings took showers with rushing water that bounced off their skin, and they brushed their teeth with harsh bristles glued to a plastic stick. Scarlet loved it all!

Dressed and ready for the journey, Scarlet took what was left of her limited time on Starland before her mission began to practice her energy manipulation. She concentrated as hard as she could, visualizing a holographic image on her dorm room wall of a perfect blue sky against a green grassy hill on an idyllic day somewhere on Wishworld. Scarlet stood in front of it to admire all its Wishworld beauty and wonder. "I'm coming to you, Wishworld! So stoked about it, too!" She grabbed her fuchsia drumsticks. "And these are definitely coming with me!"

One of the big absolute no-nos on Starland was to reveal to a Wishling that you were actually a Starling who was granting a wish. Scarlet was well aware of that rule, and wondered what it would be like to live among the Wishlings one day for real, not as a secret visitor on a mission.

Sage rushed to the mirror hanging on her lavender patterned wall, lit by a floating chandelier. She tried to imagine all the challenges that awaited her on Wishworld. "You can do this, Sage!" she said to her reflection. Then she recited her Mirror Mantra. "I believe in you. Glow for it!" She thought of the Wish Blossom she had received after her first mission to Wishworld, a boheminella that glowed with soft healing lavender light. If she completed this mission successfully, she would receive another. What an honor that would be! It was true that her mom's Wish Blossoms filled the Hall of Granted Wishes. Sage had only one blossom in the silvery garden. She longed for more, to carve out a name for herself on Starland. This Wish Mission could very well be the opportunity of her dreams.

Sage began her Wishworld cram session, speeding through the what, when, where, and how to blend in on Wishworld. It had been a while since her last mission, and she wondered how much Wishworld had changed since then. She instructed her Star-Zap to send her holograms of the latest trends and styles. Sage also pulled up a list of the most popular vocabulary words Wishlings her age used day to day.

There was a knock at her door. "Yes?" Sage asked hurriedly, busy preparing for the imminent journey to Wishworld.

"MO-J4 here, Miss Sage. May I enter?"

Her eyes remained transfixed on her Star-Zap, absorbed in all that was startrending on Wishworld. She barely acknowledged MO-J4, murmuring, "Door is open."

MO-J4 zoomed in and immediately zeroed in on Sage. "Many congratulations to you on being selected by Lady Stella to go to Wishworld for this important mission. Your star aura is shining so brightly." MO-J4 showed great enthusiasm for Sage's upcoming journey. He seemed to be as excited as she was, which was unusual for a Bot-Bot!

Sage looked up from her Star-Zap vocab search. "How are you doing since your tech rejuvenation visit?" she asked.

"Kind of you to inquire, Miss Sage. Wires

checked out just fine, as a matter of fact."

MO-J4 wasn't used to such personal questions from a Starling. Sage was oblivious to the unique way in which she treated this Bot-Bot. She talked to him almost as if he was a Starling, too.

"And no more problems with your Star-Zap?" he asked.

"Yep. Works great. Just in time, too."

MO-J4 tried to minimize his concern for Sage and her new mission. "You're ready then. Good luck, Miss Sage."

Sage looked up at MO-J4. "Thanks! I'll see you at Light Giving Day."

"That's right. You'll be back by Light Giving Day." He paused, then said, "Safe journey to you. Miss Leona and Miss Scarlet, too." Then he quickly zoomed out.

Sage didn't even hear the door close. She could only think about her mission. She stood up, walked over to the mirror, and recited her Mirror Mantra one more time. "I believe in you. Glow for it!" A rush of positive energy filled her body, head to toe. She was overwhelmed with a warm, comforting feeling that her destiny was now aligned with Starland's future, her mission part of a bigger plan.

Leona, Scarlet, Sage, and Lady Stella stood at the edge of the Wishworld Surveillance Deck, surrounded by the rest of the Star Darlings. Lady Stella checked the sky for shooting stars. There were many brightly colored stars that evening, which boded well for the mission. Two Star Wranglers stood behind her, ready to catch them for the three Starlings.

Lady Stella walked up to the raised podium and announced to the twelve Star Darlings, "We are soon approaching this important mission. Please, Leona, Scarlet, and Sage, step up to receive your Power Crystals. The Star Wranglers are ready to lasso your three stars, and then you'll be off to Wishworld."

Each Star Darling had a Power Crystal created just for her. They were now safely stored in the underground Wish Cavern on campus, but on occasions such as this one, when a Starling traveled to Wishworld, the crystals were brought out and placed on a necklace for each Starling to wear throughout the mission. Each girl's Power Crystal intensified her unique powers on Wishworld.

Lady Stella first placed Leona's glowing yellow glisten paw around the Starling's neck. It shone brightly, sending a wave of warmth into Leona. She giggled with delight.

Scarlet stepped up to the platform next to receive her Power Crystal. Her ravenstone necklace triggered a powerful surge of light throughout her whole body. She was overwhelmed by the sense of confidence she felt. She knew that this mission would be different from her last one. Something special awaited her there. She could just feel it.

Sage was the last of the trio to receive her Power Crystal. Lady Stella looked her in the eye. "This healing lavenderite will protect you, and give you the strength and power you need to stop the bad wish from being granted. It is unique to you, and it suits your powers perfectly. Sage, good luck."

When she placed the crystal necklace around Sage's neck, Sage filled with a positive glow. She smiled and bowed. "Celestial gratitude, Lady Stella."

Lady Stella stepped away from Sage. She addressed all three Star Darlings now. "Remember to be mindful of your Wish Pendants, too." As she spoke, Leona's golden metallic cuff, Scarlet's star boot buckles, and Sage's sparkling star necklace all lit up and sparkled under the starry sky. Lady Stella continued. "They will tell you if you're close to the Wisher, and they are also vessels for you to store any positive wish energy you collect on Wishworld once you have stopped the bad wish."

Vega stepped away from the others, up to the podium. She handed each Starling a pair of safety starglasses.

Lady Stella continued, more rushed now, since the Star Darlings' journey was only a few starmins away. Even though each girl had been on a Wish Mission before, she reminded them what to expect. "Remember, when you enter Wishworld's atmosphere, your Star-Zap will signal that it is time to change your appearance. You've each viewed the Wishworld Outfit Selector, so you know your fashion options. Remember that your Wishworld wardrobe will help you blend in with the Wishlings. This mission is of great importance to Starland. Your true identity must be kept a secret at all times. If you find yourself making friends or growing close to a Wishling, that is not a bad thing, but remember to stay true to your mission. *You must find and stop Vivica from granting a Wisher's bad wish.* Pay close attention to the Countdown Clock on your Star-Zap, too. The bad wish must be stopped before your collective wish energy runs out."

Lady Stella signaled to Libby, who revealed three star-shaped strapped bags, one for each Starling. As Libby handed out the bags to Leona, Sage, and Scarlet, Lady Stella further explained, "As you know, Wishlings call these bags that strap around your back *backpacks.*

Most Wishling students wear them. This will be another way for you to blend in on Wishworld. You may also use these sacks to collect useful objects and artifacts from the mission."

A Star Wrangler abruptly rushed up to Lady Stella. He whispered in her ear, pointing urgently to the sky. A shooting star began its graceful descent toward Wishworld. The timing couldn't have been more suited to catching a ride.

Lady Stella concealed her emotions and concern for the Star Darlings who were about to journey to Wishworld. She held each of the three Star Darlings' hands in her own and warned, "We will be able to monitor your wish energy reserves through your Wish Pendant. If you absolutely need to communicate with us through your Star-Zaps, you can, but each time will drain your energy reserves, so use them sparingly. Other than that, you'll be on your own once you break through the atmosphere to Wishworld."

Sage tried but was unable to contain her excitement. "To Wishworld!" she shouted.

"To Wishworld!" Leona and Scarlet echoed.

Then the Star Wranglers expertly caught three perfectly aligned shooting stars. One by one, the three Star Darlings—first Leona, then Scarlet, then Sage—hitched to their stars and rode down to Wishworld. It was time to save Starland.

CHAPTER

Seven

Wishworld at last!

A hooded figure stood before a super modern structure on a hilltop that overlooked a bustling coastal port town. Rain poured from the gray sky, where dark clouds hung overhead. It was all very mysterious.

Vivica looked around, unimpressed with the land of wishes she had heard so much about ever since she was a wee Starling. "It's raining?" she muttered as she adjusted her hood to protect her long hair. This was her very first time on Wishworld and even though she had just arrived, she was already annoyed by the downpour.

She stood under a covered area, staring at the entrance of the building, which had a sign engraved on it that read NORTH COAST PERFORM-ING ARTS CENTER. When the rain finally let up a little, the cloaked Starling dropped her hood, revealing pale almost white-blond hair, with just a lock of her Starland silvery-blue in front. Vivica lifted her hand to touch the teardrop necklace that hung around her neck, just to make sure it had survived the trip in one piece.

A small group of chatty girls hurried together to the arts center entrance. They were dressed alike, wearing identical leggings, long wooly socks and tie-up boots, bulky sweaters, and colorful scarves.

As they walked by Vivica, she quipped, "Didn't know there was a dress code here."

The leader of the small clique, Whitney, flipped her long bangs and adjusted her woolen hat. She turned to stare down Vivica. "No dress code. We all just have really good taste."

Vivica hadn't realized Wishlings would be

so smug. She hadn't learned *that* in Wishling Relations class. She knew she should slide her way out of the conversation and find her Wisher, even though she was enjoying herself. *"Excuse me*, I'm on a mission—" She stopped herself mid-sentence. She was still adjusting to being on Wishworld. Then she noticed a motivational plaque on the front wall of the building. TO BE OR NOT TO BE—THAT IS THE QUESTION. She repeated it to the girls. "I'm on a mission . . . to be or not to be."

"Okay. Weird, but okay," Whitney said, turning to her friends and making a silly face at them, mocking Vivica. They all giggled together.

Vivica hissed. "Not laughing, Wishlings."

They turned to her again. In unison, they asked, *"Wishlings?"*

Whitney rolled her eyes, then turned her back on Vivica. "Let's get to rehearsal. Wordsworth is going to kill us if we're late!"

"He's crazy strict."

"Let's get out of here." Whitney turned to peer back at Vivica, then said to her friends, "Who *is* she, anyway?"

"Don't know. Don't wanna know," replied Nelle, another girl in the group.

"Must be the new intern from down the hill. I heard Wordsworth just hired one for the Spring Variety Show," said a third girl.

Vivica overheard the girls' conversation as they walked away. She repeated to herself, "Intern. I'm the intern!" She flipped on her Star-Zap that was disguised as a Wishling cell phone and asked for a definition of the word *intern*. Her Star-Zap quickly answered: AN APPRENTICE WHO WORKS WITHOUT PAY TO GAIN EXPERIENCE. "Okay, I could totally be that."

Vivica knew it might take a little while to adjust to Wishworld. She reminded herself she was just a first-year student, so there could be a learning curve she hadn't anticipated. Still, she felt she was ready for whatever Wishworld had to offer, even this group of girls. Just for the fun of it, and to test her skills away from Starland, she levitated Whitney's water bottle from the outside pocket of the girl's backpack and poured it over her head. "Nice, Vivica," she whispered to herself.

Whitney screeched. "My new beanie is ruined!" She turned to the other girls in her posse. "What just happened?"

"No clue, but I'm seriously keeping my distance from intern girl," Nelle said.

Whitney looked at Vivica and then back to her friends, the whole time trying to fix her hair and wring out her hat.

Vivica smiled at them, then murmured to herself, "Totally love those girls. They remind me of someone." As she slipped into the arts center, she thought, *Oh, yeah . . . it's me!*

Vivica arrived on Wishworld with just a description of her Wisher from Rancora. All she had to do now was cross Clara's path, and her Star-Zap was programmed to do the rest. She followed Whitney, Nelle, and the other girls to the main theater. Just as she entered it, her teardrop necklace crackled.

Vivica took that as a good sign and slipped into the darkened theater, quickly grabbing a seat in the back row.

A man with long salt-and-pepper hair barked

at the students, "We've got a show to do, people!" Vivica realized he must be the director, Mr. Wordsworth. He was dressed in baggy jeans and a crinkled red-and-black plaid shirt. He marched down the center aisle, clapping his hands. "Actors and singers. Dancers, too. Don't try to hide from me. Why are you dancers so shy?" he asked playfully. "Time for rehearsal. Let's start with a run-through of the acts." Then he shouted, "Is my intern here?"

Whitney spotted Vivica in the back row and pointed to her. "There she is!"

Vivica quickly slipped behind a column.

"I don't see anyone," Wordsworth grumbled impatiently. "This is the theater! We don't have time for fun and games!"

Whitney looked around the room, confused. She assured the temperamental director whom she desperately wanted to impress that she was telling the truth. "She was right there!"

"I need her here, now!" the director demanded.

Vivica slunk over to another part of the theater. This time, she knew not to call too much attention to herself. She discreetly found a seat in the dark corner, where no one would notice her. She wasn't ready to play intern yet. First she wanted to find Clara.

While the director gathered the cast and crew to start leading a run-through of the show, Vivica's icy blue eyes scanned the theater for her Wisher. Her teardrop necklace crackled and sparked. She knew her Wisher was close. Her eyes darted around the room, and her heart started racing. She saw a girl sitting by herself just across the aisle. Vivica had a feeling this was Clara. The cold aching in her bones told her so.

While the other cast members sat attentively waiting for Wordsworth's next direction, the girl who Vivica guessed was Clara had separated herself from the others. She sat alone with a pair of giant headphones on.

Vivica practically flew over to Clara. Flying was fine on Starland, but Vivica reminded herself she had to act like a Wishling now. She brushed past a small group of students, leaving a stream of blue-black light, invisible to Wishlings, in her wake.

In a soft, silky voice, Vivica asked her unwitting Wisher, "Anyone sitting here?"

Clara didn't hear Vivica at first. Her headphones were still glued to her ears. She moved her head back and forth to an inaudible beat. It looked almost as if she was trying to tune out the whole world.

Vivica ran her fingers through her long hair, still adjusting to the newness of Wishworld. Her teardrop necklace sizzled and released a puff of dark smoke. Finally, Clara took off her headphones and looked in Vivica's eyes without blinking. "I haven't seen you around. Are you new here?"

"Yeah, I just kind of arrived in town a little while ago," Vivica said as calmly she could. "Is anyone sitting here?" she asked in a soothing tone.

Clara responded warmly, "No, have a seat. Welcome to Port Harbor."

"Thanks," Vivica said, wondering just how long the negative energy stored in her teardrop pendant would remain active and powerful. She knew it would slowly dissipate if she didn't grant the bad wish soon. But before she could grant the wish, she needed to earn her Wisher's trust.

A stagehand, dressed all in black, stealthily wheeled in a piano, while another stagehand also dressed in black brought out a microphone and adjusted it. Wordsworth stepped onstage and tapped the microphone to test the volume. He cleared his throat loudly to get everyone's attention and waited for the students to quiet down. "I have an important announcement to make," he began. "I guess word has gotten out that this theater has some incredible talent, because I learned yesterday that a producer from one of the biggest singing competitions on TV will be at our show on opening night!"

He waited a beat as the news sunk in. The room echoed with shrieks of joy and chatter as the students buzzed to each other about the news, guessing which show it could be. Whitney shouted out to Wordsworth, "Which show is it?"

"It's *Song and Chance*," he replied, and he couldn't help cracking a small smile as the room once again erupted with excitement.

Vivica had obviously never heard of the show, but she could tell from the look on Clara's face and the others' reactions that it was a huge deal.

"They're scouting talent for their televised auditions," Wordsworth added. Before his performers could completely spiral out of control, the director clapped his hands for attention and spoke loudly into the mic. "Students! If you want to impress this producer, let's run through the show—now! I must figure out the timing and best order for the acts." He was all business. "Miss Holly, why don't you try out your song? Let's hear what you prepared for the variety show. I'm sure it's as spectacular as ever."

A bubbly blond student stepped onstage. She wore her hair in an oversized side braid with a ribbon woven into it. Even Vivica was taken in by the girl's natural charisma. She stopped talking to Clara the moment the girl stepped up to the microphone. Clara turned away from Vivica, sighed, and put on her headphones again.

Vivica turned back to her Wisher. "Who's

that?" she asked. She could almost guess the answer, but she wanted to hear it from Clara herself.

Clara took off her headphones. "You say something?"

Vivica pointed to Holly onstage. "Who's that?" she repeated.

Clara took a long deep breath. "You really did just arrive here. That's Holly. And knowing her, I'm sure she'll get that television producer's attention." Clara's eyes drifted toward the stage, where Holly was just about to finish the romantic pop ballad. "She's supposedly my best friend, but I'm kinda over her lately."

Vivica's necklace crackled and vibrated. She had already found the Wisher, Clara, and now here was the Wisher's best friend, the one who clearly inspired Clara's jealous feelings. Vivica was pleased with herself. Now she just had to figure out how to help Clara push Holly out of the spotlight.

CHAPTER

Eight

As Sage, Leona, and Scarlet careened through space, bright stars whooshed past them. The pure beauty of this particular sky caught all three Star Darlings by surprise. The Starlings had each traveled to Wishworld before, but they hadn't remembered the trip being as magnificent as this one. Perhaps it had something to do with three Starlings traveling together. Up until then, it had only been one Star Darling at a time journeying to Wishworld on each Wish Mission. That must explain the triple-powered glow of lavenders, golds, and bright pinks that painted the sky.

The Star Darlings passed unfamiliar celestial constellations and extraordinary star formations that they had never seen before, and soon it was time for them to chant the transformational words before entering Wishworld's atmosphere. They spread their arms out wide and reached for each other's hands, then held them tightly against the rushing and swirling wind.

Together, they recited, "Star light, star bright, the first star I see tonight: I wish I may, I wish I might, have the wish I wish tonight."

As they entered Wishworld's atmosphere, each transformed from a sparkling and vibrant-colored Starling to an adorable Wishling teenager. They looked like themselves, minus the visible shine and sparkle, although they all still glowed from the inside. Leona's golden mane turned into wavy chestnut-brown locks. The Wishworld Outfit Selector provided the washed bell-bottom jeans and flowery peasant blouse Leona had pre-selected, plus the sweetest pair of tan suede fringed ankle boots. Scarlet was a brunette, and her outfit suited her perfectly: a pair of dark pink skinny jeans with black leather chunky boots and a graphic skater T-shirt. Sage's hair was light brown and wavy, and she wore a flowy spaghetti-strapped dress with a white shirt underneath, and a pair of platform sneakers. The Star Darlings were ready to make their entrance.

Any sign of glimmer on the Starlings' hair or skin had completely vanished, with only a colorful streak remaining in each of their new hairstyles: lavender for Sage, gold for Leona, and fuchsia for Scarlet. Their skin dulled and their auras disappeared temporarily. They each watched in awe as the others became Wishlings before their eyes. They knew the Wish Mission that lay ahead would be challenging, and so much depended on all three of them for its success, but they couldn't stop themselves from enjoying the sheer thrill of returning to Wishworld.

Now they were almost there. With their backpacks on and their Wish Pendants and Power Crystals in place, they prepared to arrive on Wishworld.

The three Star Darlings' Star-Zaps lit up all at

once. In a chorus of light, they flashed: PREPARE FOR LANDING.

It was time!

⌒

The Starlings tumbled onto the soft, grassy Wishworld ground. They had landed in a small coastal city named Port Harbor, but they didn't have a clue where Vivica or the Wisher would be found.

Sage covered her head from the rain with her backpack. "I see something over there," she said, pointing to a modern building with a cement roof tilted at an angle. It almost looked like it was a sculpture.

Leona twirled dramatically, sniffing the damp, cool Wishworld air. "We're not on Starland anymore, that's for sure."

She and Sage ran across the squishy grass toward the building, but Scarlet preferred to take her time. She breathed in the fresh air, relishing the smell of the tall pine trees that reached high into the sky and lined the hillside. She glanced toward the horizon and saw an endless body of water with a quaint small town bordering the shore. "That must be the ocean!" she gasped, finding it hard to contain her excitement.

Sage and Leona made it to the side entrance of the modern building. Leona shivered. "I'm soaked. We need to find a place to stay before we start looking for Vivica and the Wisher."

Sage spotted a door with a sign made of corrugated metal hanging over it that read NORTH COAST PERFORMING ARTS CENTER. "It's the arts center that the Wisher attends, the one Lady Stella briefed us about," Sage said. Her eyes sparkled.

Thrilled that the Star Darlings were on track, Leona exclaimed, "We're here!"

Scarlet joined Sage and Leona, and the girls cautiously stepped inside the building. Drenched down to their new Wishling boots, they sloshed down the main hallway.

"Wherever Vivica is, the Wisher cannot be far behind," Sage said. She adjusted her backpack and checked her Star-Zap. With a look of concern, she told Leona and Scarlet, "Our wish energy is already starting to drain."

Leona ran her hands through her curly

Wishling hair, still getting used to it. "I've got to get to a mirror pronto and fix myself up before I make my re-debut into Wishworld."

Sage scouted the hallway. "Where do you think we can find a good place to stay while we're on our mission?"

Scarlet had broken away from the other Star Darlings, veering off down a side hallway. She used her special Wishworld power, which was gravitational pull, to unlock a bolted door to a storage room. With a clear mind and pure focus, Scarlet could unlock doors by mentally manipulating the locks. She could also make heavy things suddenly feel light as a feather. Scarlet called the other Star Darlings over to her. "Come quick!" She waved to them, then led the way inside the dusty room. "How about here?" Scarlet asked casually.

Sage and Leona entered the small, crowded room. Sage looked around, checking out every corner. It was a mess of old costumes, props, and broken stage furniture, but there were a couple of big soft couches, and they could tidy it up a bit. She hugged Scarlet enthusiastically. "It looks like nobody ever comes in here. It's perfect!"

Scarlet shied away from Sage, uncomfortable with her exuberant hug. She folded her arms in front of her chest. "Okay, cool. This will be home base."

"This place is a Wishworld fashion gold mine!" Leona squealed. She scoured the room that overflowed with a seemingly endless supply of wardrobe pieces and accessories, all from past theatrical productions. She had set her sights on finding a mirror. Instead, she found an old bejeweled king's robe. She wrapped it around herself and danced around the cluttered storage room.

Scarlet just shook her head. *It's always a show for Leona,* she thought. "We're on a mission, remember?" she reminded her fellow Starling. "This time it's not about *you*."

"Just getting myself used to Wishworld again," Leona said, ignoring Scarlet's criticism. She spotted a small-framed mirror hanging at the far end of the storage room. "Super!" Posing with the royal robe, she playfully admired herself from every angle. "I really *am* fabulous wherever I go!"

Scarlet rolled her eyes and found a corner of an old torn red velvet couch to rest on; she was a little tired after the long trip from Starland.

Sage immediately thought about the Star Darlings' next step. She knew that, for this Wish Mission, each Starling had to be at her very best, inside and out. It had been an exhilarating light-filled journey, and the Star Darlings needed time to recharge before taking their next step, but Sage wasn't going to let Scarlet and Leona's squabbling get in the way.

Scarlet leaned back on the vintage couch, relieved to be back on Wishworld. "Nice to breathe Wishworld air again, even if we are stuck in this stuffy old closet!" she mused.

Leona ignored Scarlet and babbled on. "So many new wardrobe options. Loving it here already . . ." When she discovered an emerald taffeta gown and a feather boa, she threw off the king's robe and wrapped the boa around her neck. "I could make this work, too!" she exclaimed.

Scarlet covered her eyes with her hands, bemoaning the fact that out of all the other Star Darlings Lady Stella could have chosen for this Wish Mission, the headmistress had selected her roommate, Leona. She knew she'd have to tolerate her in the name of Starland, but still. It seemed as though fate was playing a little trick on her.

Sage was too busy pacing around the room and zeroing in on their mission to even notice what Leona was doing. "We've got to get started like right now! Our combined wish energy will only take us so far." She scanned the walls for a clue as to where to begin. Sage noticed an assortment of posters with affirmations: DREAM BIG; ART CHANGES EVERYTHING; OKAY, NOW DANCE! Next to those, almost hidden by a rack of hats, something else caught her eye. A map of the building!

"Found something!" Sage exclaimed as she pulled the map from the wall and started studying it. "Leona, Scarlet, come check this out." Sage's acute mental powers meant she could absorb information with great speed, which allowed her to memorize the layout of the arts center in a single glance. The center's layout was a branching web of hallways all leading to a prominent main theater. "Vivica and the Wisher could be anywhere in the building," she said to the other two Star Darlings. "It would be best for us to split up."

Leona squinted as she took a closer look at the map. She sprang up. "I'll cover the dance studio. Need to do some stretching and warmups anyway after that shooting star ride."

"I didn't know dancing was on the agenda for saving Starland," Scarlet said bitingly to Leona.

Leona was used to Scarlet's sarcasm, so she just ignored it. "The Wisher might be in the dance studio! Plus, I totally need to stay on top of my game to overpower Vivica, and dance keeps me on my toes!" She smiled.

Scarlet raised her eyebrows. "Whatever, Leona." She glanced down at the map. "I'll check out the rehearsal rooms. I'm pretty decent at unlocking doors, so if Vivica or the Wisher is in one of the rooms, I'll find her." Just for fun, she moved the chaise in the corner of the room that Leona was about to sit on clear across the room. Leona almost fell to the floor, but caught herself in time.

"Scarlet!" Leona shrieked, straightening out her new Wishling clothes and hair. "So unnecessary."

"Just fine-tuning my skills for the mission. *I totally need to stay on top of my game to overpower Vivica,*" Scarlet replied, mocking Leona.

Trying to contain her exasperation, Sage wondered just how long Leona and Scarlet's quibbling would last. Did she have to remind them they were on a mission, not hanging out in their dorm room arguing over who took longer sparkle showers or whose side of the room was messier? Sage knew Lady Stella was counting on her to lead the mission and make sure the bad wish wasn't granted. She wanted more than anything to prove that her headmistress was right to trust her.

She pointed to the center's map. "There! That's where I'm going. To the main theater!"

"Well, I'm ready," Leona sang out.

Scarlet stood up from the couch. "I am, too."

"Then we've got a plan!" Sage said. "Since we're splitting up, we'll need to stay on our Star-Zaps at all times. And, really important—no matter what happens, absolutely no Wishworld distractions!"

Leona nodded in agreement and repeated, "No Wishworld distractions!"

Sage looked over to Scarlet, who seemed to be in her own world. "Scarlet, are you there?"

"No Wishworld distractions. Check," Scarlet said slowly.

All three Star Darlings stepped out into the hallway with a single purpose. Sage looked at Leona and Scarlet with determination and focus. "Mission to save Starland commencing right now." The Star Darlings put their hands in together, then brought them apart and into the air like a starburst. "To Starland!"

CHAPTER

Nine

Did someone say "fabulous Wishling in the house"?
Leona thought as she strutted down the arts center main hallway with Scarlet and Sage. *I feel so entirely Wishling, I might even fool myself!*

Whitney, Nelle, and the rest of their girl crew instantly took notice of Leona's dramatic entrance. They sashayed toward the Star Darlings in one tightly knit group, almost as if they were stuck to one another.

Whitney pointed to the streak in Leona's hair and called out, "What's that, new girl?"

"Hi, I'm Leona. What's *what*?" Leona asked,

trying to figure out a way to somehow avoid the question.

Scarlet bowed her head, hoping to make herself disappear, which on Wishworld was impossible. She knew that, of course, but she tried anyway. "Did you really have to call that much attention to yourself?" Scarlet whispered to Leona.

Sage agreed with Scarlet. Lady Stella had made it very clear that maintaining the Star Darlings' secret identity was of utmost importance to the success of the Wish Mission. Sage was about to remind Leona about the sensitive nature of their visit, when the group of girls moved in even closer and surrounded the three Star Darlings.

"You need to tell us who did your hair, like right now," Nelle demanded.

Pointing to Sage, Whitney gushed, "That shade of lavender in your streak is something I don't think I've ever seen before. It's *amaze*!"

Sage felt her face warming. She must have been "blushing." That's what Wishlings called it, anyway. On Starland, whenever a Starling was overcome by feelings of embarrassment and didn't know what to say, she simply glowed brighter than usual. On Wishworld, Wishlings apparently turned a bright shade of red and their faces heated up!

Racking her brain, Sage tried to figure out if *amaze* was a good thing or a bad thing. She quickly went through all the slang words she had pulled up on her Star-Zap when she'd been studying Wishworld vocabulary words, but she didn't remember seeing that one. From the looks on the faces of the enthusiastic group of girls, Sage guessed it was a good thing.

"Amaze to you, too," she told the girls.

Whitney enjoyed Sage's awkward attempt at fitting in. "You're so cute, you just don't seem real!"

Another girl in the group eyed Sage, Leona, and Scarlet standing together. "Hold up." She backed away from them to get a better view of all three Star Darlings. She noticed Scarlet's fuchsia streak now. "All three of you have streaks in your hair. What's going on with that?"

Sage covered her face with her hands. She

couldn't believe they had aroused so much suspicion so soon into the mission.

Then Whitney shouted, "I love it!" The rest of the Wishling girls all laughed together. The Star Darlings didn't understand the Wishling humor, but they were relieved and laughed along with them. It was their attempt to blend in with the students.

It turned out Wishlings were more trusting than Professor Margaret Dumarre had led them to believe in their Wishworld Relations class. Not only did the Wishlings believe that the colorful streaks in the Starlings' hair were fashion statements, they also couldn't wait to get theirs colored exactly the same way.

Leona turned to her friends and whispered, "We're trendsetters! How cool is that?" Sage breathed a huge sigh of relief. Their identities were still safe.

After-school performance workshops of all creative disciplines were fully under way at the bustling arts center. Dancing, singing, acting, drumming, piano-playing, chorus. It was all happening. Creativity burst from every direction and from behind every rehearsal room door. The Star Darlings agreed they would stay in touch on their Star-Zaps, and made a plan to split up and then meet back at the storage room in one hour.

"Deep breaths, Starlings," Sage told Leona and Scarlet. "Deep breaths."

Scarlet glided down a long hallway of practice rooms. From behind the closed doors, she heard the muffled sounds of young musicians practicing their instruments. There were the low tones of a French horn and trombone flowing from one room, and the high-pitched notes of a pair of flutes from another room. The beautiful cacophony of sounds made Scarlet miss playing her own music with the Star Darlings band. She felt most content—most *Scarlet*—when she was sitting at her drums, lost in a song. Music helped her feel less of an outsider and more connected to herself and her bandmates. She reached into her backpack to check that her favorite drumsticks were safely tucked inside. She had brought the drumsticks all the way to Wishworld with her as good luck charms.

Scarlet breezed by a practice room that appeared to be empty. She used her special powers to unlock it and slipped inside. Savoring the quiet of the room, Scarlet inhaled deeply. When she turned on the lights, standing before her was a drum set, as if it was just waiting for her!

She peeked out the door and down the hall to check if any students were coming. All the student musicians were busy practicing in their own rooms. The hall was empty. Confident she was alone, Scarlet sat down at the drums, pulled out her hot-pink drumsticks that had traveled so far, and started to play.

Soon she got lost in the rhythms. She felt overwhelmed by the thoughts rushing through her head. She was on a crucial Wish Mission, yet she couldn't help having the feeling of wanting to escape it all. If only she could really take time to explore the wonders of Wishworld and what this special place had to offer her. The training at Starling Academy had prepared her for this mission, but it hadn't prepared her for the rest-less feelings inside.

She soon let those thoughts pass and got lost in her drumming. All of a sudden, she felt a tap on her shoulder. She leaped off the drum throne, pointing her drumsticks at the intruder and pre-pared to use them as weapons. "What is going on?" Scarlet asked, trying to assess the situation, channeling all of the education that had led her to this Wish Mission.

A cute Wishling boy had his hands up, in an exaggerated gesture meant to convey inno-cence. "I was going to ask you the same thing." He smiled, then took a closer look at Scarlet and the drumsticks she was pointing at him. "Please don't hurt me, I'm just a trumpet player."

Are his eyes especially green? Scarlet won-dered as she looked at him. Then, shaking off the thought, she quickly found the words to answer him. "I, uh, was just leaving. Sorry about that." She put the sticks in her backpack and made a beeline for the door. Something about this Wishling threw her off her game, but she knew better than to overreact. *You belong here,*

Scarlet. You're a "Wishling," too, remember? She was trained for situations just like this one. Why had this boy frazzled her?

"Wait," he said. "I didn't catch your name."

"That's because I didn't throw it to you."

He laughed. "Okay, so . . . ?"

"So?" Scarlet stalled while she tried to figure out what to do next. She didn't want to rush out of the room too quickly, for fear of raising suspicions.

"You're right. I should introduce myself first. Let's start again." He promptly left the room and then walked back inside. This time he offered his hand for Scarlet to shake. "Hi. I haven't seen you around here and I wondered what your name is?"

"And?" Scarlet asked, trying to find a way out of this awkward conversation as quickly as possible.

The boy seemed to enjoy Scarlet's impertinence, although that wasn't her intention. "My name is Maxwell. What's yours?"

Why was he so insistent on knowing Scarlet's name? Her heart fluttered so fast it echoed throughout her body. *Wishlings shouldn't have this kind of effect on a Starling*, she thought. It went against what she had studied on Starland. She was feeling weird. She rushed out of the room without speaking another word.

Just then, Scarlet's Star-Zap flashed. Sage needed her to go to the main theater right away. Sage had spotted Vivica *and* the Wisher. As Scarlet raced down the hall, she reminded herself, *Boys are just distractions. I'm on a Wish Mission to save Starland, hello?*

"And one, and two, and three . . ." Pete, the choreographer, called out to a class of fifteen Wishling dancers . . . plus Leona! Leona thought of herself as a decent dancer on Starland, but standing in the middle of a Wishling dance studio trying to keep up with the gifted ballerinas in the room proved to be a challenge. She couldn't give up now, since *blending in* meant not calling too much attention to herself. She had promised Sage and Scarlet she would stay focused on the mission no matter what.

Pirouette? Pas de deux? These were terms she

had never heard of up on Starland. Dance on her home star was more free-form, more improvisational. There weren't names for moves. What was she supposed to do now?

Pete wove through the group of dancers. "Dancers, over to the wall. We're going to take it one at a time across the room," he commanded.

Leona counted out the steps in her head. "One, and two, and . . ." Just when it was her turn to dance the combination in front of the whole class, her Star-Zap flashed.

The choreographer had a no-phone policy in the classroom, so he was furious with her. "Shut it off," Pete said, glaring at Leona.

She used the special persuasive power Starlings have over Wishling adults to her advantage and told him, "I have to go somewhere right now. It's okay with you." Pete responded by opening his arms and saying in a soft, patient voice, "You've got to do whatever you need to do. It's okay with me."

Leona raced across the floor and grabbed her backpack. Looking back around the room, she said sheepishly, "Family emergency!"

The class fell silent and so did the choreographer, who gave her a sympathetic look. He said, "Go on, honey. Family is everything."

Leona waved good-bye to him and the other dancers. "So true!"

She turned the corner and holo-texted Sage: WHAT'S UP?

I HAVE VIVICA AND THE WISHER IN MY SIGHTS. GET TO THE MAIN THEATER NOW! DO YOU HAVE ANY IDEA WHERE SCARLET IS?

Just then Scarlet turned the corner and appeared right next to Leona. "Scarlet!" Leona screamed.

Scarlet hushed Leona. "We talked about not making a scene, remember?" She grabbed Leona's hand. "I know. We need to get to the theater. Come on. Let's go!"

CHAPTER
Ten

Vivica!

Sage spotted Vivica from behind, so luckily Vivica hadn't seen her. Vivica's transformation into a pale-haired Wishworld teen, dressed in all black, with spiky heels and bright blue nail polish had thrown Sage for a moment. But as Sage got closer and saw the silvery-blue streak in her hair, discreetly tucked behind her ear, she knew it was Vivica. And she knew the girl was with the Wisher.

Lady Stella hadn't known how much negative energy had overtaken Vivica's body, so it was nearly impossible to determine the extent of its power. Sage waited anxiously for Leona and Scarlet to get to the theater. She suspected that she wouldn't be able to confront Vivica alone. Why else would Lady Stella have sent three Star Darlings for this Wish Mission?

She hid toward the end of a side row in the darkened theater with her eyes fixed on Vivica and Clara, who sat next to each other while other acts rehearsed onstage. Vivica still hadn't noticed Sage. She was too busy stealing all of Clara's attention. The two were friends now, apparently, and Vivica was trying to find a way to understand more about the bad wish and win Clara's trust with her charms.

Clara smiled. "I've never had a friend like you, Vivica. You seem to be so interested in me." Her eyes glazed over as she looked at Vivica.

"I can almost guarantee you won't ever have a friend like me again." Vivica's necklace sparked, but as a Wishling, Clara couldn't see the sparks. However, the negative energy had already had an effect on her.

Now that Clara was under the spell of the

negativity, Vivica began to transform and cloud Clara's perspective. She started by convincing her that Holly had never been a good friend to her and zapping any good memories that Clara had of her friendship with Holly. As long as the negative power in Vivica's necklace remained strong, Clara was no longer completely in control of her own thoughts.

Vivica's necklace continued to sizzle. She manipulated Clara by pointing to Holly, who was standing nearby, surrounded by Whitney and her girl clique.

Holly noticed Clara looking her way. She waved to her, but with Vivica's negative forces at work, Clara saw the friendly gesture as fake. Clara turned away, annoyed, and Holly turned back to the group of girls, visibly hurt by Clara's dismissal.

Whitney, Nelle, and the rest of the girls were circling Holly, admiring just about everything about her.

"How do you do that braid? You always have such cool braids and hairstyles. You need to vlog about it," Whitney insisted.

"Agreed! A vlog! That's perfect. I would totally follow you!" Nelle affirmed.

"We know, Nelle." Whitney smiled and turned to Holly. "We all want to be there when you're a star on *Song and Chance*! Promise?"

Holly blushed and hid her face. "Come on, you guys! Anyone here could get picked for the show, not just me." As both girls vied for Holly's attention, all Holly could think of was how her best friend was no longer talking to her.

Vivica pointed to Holly, working her negative influence over Clara. "Look how much she enjoys being the center of attention. She doesn't even care that you're sitting over here."

Clara agreed. "You're right. She's not even looking at me. I don't know how I'd handle this without you."

Vivica sensed an opening to further influence her Wisher. She had succeeded in gaining Clara's trust, and now she needed to figure out how she could guide Clara toward actually making her bad wish come true.

Leona and Scarlet entered the darkened theater, undetected by Vivica. Luckily, the only light in the large theater was onstage. Sage spotted her friends and immediately waved them over to her. They snuck around the edge of the theater to the back row.

Wordsworth shouted to the booth at the back of the balcony. "Lighting team. Spotlight over here, please!"

All three Star Darlings ducked down out of view as the spotlight panned the audience. Vivica turned in the direction of the Star Darlings. She still didn't see them, but she didn't have to, either. This time she sensed their presence. Her highly tuned intuition told her that a Star Darling was nearby. Under her breath, she taunted, "Welcome to Wishworld, Star Dipper!"

Sage, Leona, and Scarlet stayed hidden behind the seats. None of them spoke to one another, even after all three of their Wish Pendants flashed. They all felt the same thing:

Vivica knows we're here!

Sage quickly brought the Star Darlings up to speed on what she had observed so far. In a hushed whisper, she told them, "Vivica has some sort of negative hold over this girl, whose name is Clara. I've been watching them both. It's like Clara is under a spell. We need to find a way to get to Clara before Vivica helps her make the bad wish come true!"

All charged up, Leona explained that she could use her Wishworld power, which was super-hearing, to eavesdrop on Vivica and Clara's conversation. "I'll find out what the bad wish is and what they're going to do!"

Sage nodded. "Sounds like a plan."

Scarlet agreed. "Good luck, Leona." Scarlet caught herself softening toward her roommate and quickly shook herself out of it. What was happening? Could Wishworld be changing her?

Leona wasn't used to Scarlet being so encouraging. It threw her for a moment, but she quickly got back to focusing on the mission. She closed her eyes, touching behind her ears with each of her hands, and then zeroed in on Vivica and Clara. She listened for a few starmins, then turned back to the Star Darlings.

Sage leaned over to her. "What are they saying?" she asked anxiously.

"Nothing!" Leona whispered.

Sage lifted her head to observe Vivica and Clara. They were engaged in lively conversation. "I can see them talking. They can't be saying *nothing*!"

Leona opened her eyes wide and motioned to Sage to quiet her. "Wait, I hear something. It's just not coming in clearly. Let me try again."

Rehearsal would be over soon. It was crucial to get wish-granting information from Vivica and Clara while the Star Darlings had them in view. "We don't have much time, Leona!" Sage whispered urgently.

Scarlet leaned in closer. "We can't hide behind these seats too much longer without a Wishling catching on and wondering what we're doing."

Leona waved at both Sage and Scarlet to stop talking. "I've got something. Shh!" Leona closed her eyes. Then she opened them again and held her ears. "It's just noise!" Suddenly, she jumped, screeching. "Ouch! Sounds like a Bot-Bot that needs retuning!"

Sage slumped down, a bit defeated. "Must be the negative energy field that Vivica created around them. She's stronger than I thought she'd be." She tapped her head a few times with her finger. "Think, Sage, think."

Scarlet stretched her legs and then finally stood up, tired of hiding from Vivica—especially since Vivica obviously knew they were there. She immediately caught Vivica's eye and casually waved at her. Vivica casually waved back. Both played it cool. None of the Wishlings in the theater noticed anything strange, since the theater was still dark, and Vivica and Scarlet appeared to be normal teenage girls just waving at each other. The possibility that they could be Starlings representing good and evil, who held the future of their home star in their hands, never crossed any of the Wishlings' minds.

Scarlet kept her eyes locked on Vivica and Clara. Out of the corner of her mouth, hardly moving her lips, she told Leona and Sage, "She sees me. Now it's my turn to try something."

Sage checked her Star-Zap for any indication of the Star Darlings' positive energy levels. As she suspected, the levels were dwindling. She looked up at Scarlet. "It's all you. How can we help?"

Scarlet, usually defiantly independent, surprised Sage and Leona by asking them both to follow her. "Come on! And stay close."

Leona looked at Sage. Sage just shrugged and followed Scarlet. Leona was right behind her.

Wordsworth stood onstage, giving final directions to the lighting designers before rehearsal ended. "Spotlight, over here." The spotlight shifted, nearly exposing the Star Darlings as they headed down the aisle toward Vivica and Clara. They ducked just in time. "I'm thinking of the first act opening from the audience!" Wordsworth shouted, pointing to Vivica's seat. "Right about there." The spotlight shone directly on Vivica and Clara!

The Star Darlings, led by Scarlet, snuck farther down the aisle. "I'll take care of Vivica while you two grab Clara's attention and get her away from Vivica," Scarlet ordered.

Wordsworth instructed the lighting student on the spotlight. "Okay, shut it down. We've got it."

With the spotlight turned off, Scarlet moved closer to Vivica and applied her ability to manipulate gravity to try to lift Vivica off her seat, but Vivica held on to the armrests. Her necklace crackled and vibrated. The negatites were still strong. Scarlet tried again but had no power over Vivica. As Scarlet walked away, Vivica turned and shot her a nasty smirk.

Meanwhile, Clara had put her headphones back on and was listening to the song she had written to perform for the show, unaware of the struggle right next to her. But the Star Darlings could see there was a force at work that none of them had prepared for on Starland.

Scarlet returned to her friends. Out of breath, she apologized. "I tried, it just wasn't happening."

Leona reassured her. "No worries. We'll figure it out!"

Suddenly, the lights flickered on and off. Wordsworth announced the end of rehearsal. "That's a wrap. I don't need to remind you that the show is three days away. Bring your best stuff tomorrow! Now get some rest."

Just as the lights went on, Sage pointed to the spot where Clara had been sitting with Vivica. "They're gone!"

Then Scarlet noticed a girl standing at the center of the adoring group of girls led by Whitney and Nelle. "Who's she?" Scarlet asked Sage.

Sage recognized the Wishling girl. She could feel her Wish Pendant glowing. "Wait, I saw Clara and Vivica looking at her just before you and Leona arrived. The girl waved at Clara from across the theater, but Clara ignored her and turned away. I didn't think anything of it at the time, but now, maybe she's . . ."

"Part of the bad wish," Leona said, finishing Sage's thought for her.

"Yes! Let's find out more!" Sage said, gaining momentum, convinced she was closer to understanding the true nature of the bad wish. Her intuition told her that the girl would play a role in the Wish Mission, but she wasn't sure how yet. Sage noticed that the girl had a special glow about her, not the shimmering glow that Starlings had on Starland, but another kind, like she was shining from the inside. As they got closer to her, all three of their pendants glowed.

Before the Star Darlings could reach her, the

girl left the auditorium. Scarlet slipped out after her.

Leona and Sage weren't as lucky. Whitney and Nelle spotted them and waved them over. They were all wearing different-colored streaks in their hair. Leona smiled, seeing how the trends she had set were taking off on Wishworld. She pointed to Whitney's bright red streak. "Like the hair!"

Nelle showed off her lime-green streak, twirling it around her finger. "Thanks for the inspiration, new girl!"

Sage had had enough small talk and wanted answers. "So who's the girl you were talking to a minute ago?"

Nelle laughed. "You're joking, right? Everyone knows *Holly*. She's only the most amazing singer at North Coast."

"Well, her best friend, Clara, is also really good," Whitney added.

Nelle rolled her eyes. "Holly is a triple threat!" she explained to the girls.

Leona's jaw dropped. "A threat? *Holly* is a threat?" That was all the Star Darlings needed right then. Another threat! Leona couldn't believe what she was hearing.

Nelle chimed in excitedly, "Holly is a true star!"

"Only the brightest star at the North Coast Performing Arts Center. She's so ridiculously awesome, I can't even tell you," Whitney said.

Sage stepped in just in time. She instantly put all the cramming she had done for Wishling Vocabulary to work. She told the Wishling girls, "Yeah, I heard she's *amaze*?" She winked at Leona, which helped Leona find her footing again. Sage understood Wishling vocabulary better than any Starling at the academy. She whispered to Leona, "A triple threat is a person who has three different talents."

Sage managed to step away from the girls and pulled Leona aside. "Okay, so back to our mission. We know Vivica is helping guide Clara to a bad wish. And I'm pretty sure that the bad wish is about Holly!"

"For sure," Leona said. "Why else would our pendants glow?"

The girls looked at each other, running

through their heads everything they had learned about the Wishlings.

"What did Holly do to Clara? I thought they were best friends," Leona remarked.

Sage paused, then gasped. "I've got it!" Leona raised her eyebrows, eager to know what she was thinking. Sage slowly explained. "Holly and Clara are both singers and best friends. Right? But everyone around here thinks Holly is a superstar. Imagine how that would make you feel if you were Clara."

"It would make me crazy!" Leona cried.

"Exactly!" Sage said. "It's made her jealous and resentful of her very best friend! Clara has been living in Holly's shadow, and now she wants Holly to fail somehow, so she can shine."

Scarlet had walked around the exterior of the building and finally located Holly. She leaned against a wall, studying Holly's every move and not letting her out of her sight.

Scarlet noticed that Holly appeared to be waiting for someone. Then Scarlet's heart skipped a beat when the cute boy she had been talking to earlier, Maxwell, showed up and gave Holly a big hug before they walked off together.

"Okay, Wishling boy. If you want to play, let's play!" Just for fun, Scarlet decided to use her powers on Maxwell. As he walked down the sidewalk with Holly, away from the arts center building, Scarlet pointed her finger at him and tripped him. He caught himself just before he fell. Holly leaned over to him to see if he was okay. Maxwell glanced over his shoulder and saw Scarlet, away from the crowd of other students, with a smile on her face.

"Hi, there. It's you!" he called to her, collecting himself. Then he said, "Have you met my sister, Holly?"

Scarlet looked straight into Maxwell's green eyes, confused and relieved. "Your sister?"

CHAPTER

Eleven

DAY TWO

Scarlet wasn't feeling *herself*. Maybe the journey from Starland was catching up with her, or maybe it was the failed attempt to overpower Vivica's negatites. From the moment she had woken up that morning, it was like she had flutterfocuses in her stomach. She felt almost light-headed.

As she sat under a giant tree, she heard a cheerful voice. "You showed! I wondered if you actually would," Maxwell called out. He jumped on his skateboard and rode toward Scarlet, flipping the board over twice in a row and then landing back on it. He kicked the board up to his hands and stood in front of her, smiling.

Scarlet searched for even the simplest of words and could only get out "hello."

"Hey," Max said.

Then neither knew what to say for an uncomfortable moment—until Max jumped in.

"So, I bet you go to Danforth High, right? It seems like that's where all the cool girls go."

"No, I'm from a bit farther away than Danforth," Scarlet replied, feeling unusually shy.

"That explains it. I knew you seemed different."

"Thanks?" Scarlet said, wondering whether he meant "different" as a compliment. Scarlet wasn't used to second-guessing herself. She reminded herself that she was on a Wish Mission and couldn't let herself get distracted. Maxwell could provide key information about Holly for the mission. That was why Scarlet had agreed to meet up with him.

"Wherever you're from, it must be a pretty awesome place." Maxwell grinned and put down his skateboard. "You skate?"

Scarlet couldn't wait to jump back on a skateboard. Skateboarding was one of her favorite ways to escape on Starland besides playing drums. Now she had the opportunity to skateboard on Wishworld. It was almost too perfect. "I love to skate," she told him.

Maxwell grabbed her hand and led her away from the front entrance of the arts center. "I know the best skate park in Port Harbor. Let me show you."

Whisked away to a hidden skate park near the arts center, Scarlet didn't hesitate to show Maxwell her skills. It felt great to be back on a skateboard again, especially under a Wishworld sky, even if it was cloudy. The dampness in the air inspired her and made her feel as if she might be moving closer to her dream of someday living on Wishworld. First she kick-flipped the board, popped, slid, and jumped. Then she twirled around on one wheel and raised her fist in the air. "Yes!"

"Gnarly! You really aren't from around here."

He smiled. "I don't even think you're from this planet!"

"Thanks," Scarlet said, and thought, *If he only knew!* She smiled at Maxwell, who looked at her adoringly. It made her feel uneasy, even slightly nervous. She stretched herself to try another kick-flip. That time, she took a hard fall.

Maxwell ran to her to make sure she was okay. "Hey, I don't want anything to happen to you. I just met you. Tell me that you're fine."

Embarrassed and a little sore, she looked up at him. "I'm fine." She tried to get up by herself but was shaken.

Maxwell reached for her hand and held it tightly, then guided her to a nearby bench. "You're not as tough as you think you are, Scarlet who is not from around here."

Scarlet hung back and rested on the bench while Maxwell took his turn on the skateboard. He pulled off some killer tricks. After he landed a kick-flip and a backside tailslide, Scarlet shouted to him, "You're almost as good as I am!"

Maxwell shouted back, "Hey, you hungry? Want to grab something to eat downtown?"

It occurred to Scarlet that would be the most perfect opportunity to explore Wishworld, a firsthand look at that wonderfully mysterious world, and from a Wishling's point of view, too. She couldn't believe how much she was enjoying spending time with Maxwell. He was like no boy she had ever met before, nothing like the Starling boys at Star Preparatory, who thought she was strange. She was in the unusual position of liking a boy. Nothing in her Wishling Ways class had prepared her for what she was feeling— not even a little bit. She glanced at her Star-Zap and saw that her wish energy had dramatically dipped since the last time she had checked it. Not good. She quickly picked up her backpack and put it on. "Can't. I've got to get back."

Maxwell didn't understand her mood change. "What? Where? Is it something I said?" he asked.

"I, uh, just have to go." *Focus, Scarlet, focus.* In her haste, her drumsticks fell out of her backpack and rolled across the ground. She raced to grab them, but Maxwell was there first to retrieve them.

He took a close look. "Where did you get

these? I've never seen drumsticks like this before."

Scarlet grabbed them from Maxwell before he could examine them more closely. "I need those. They mean a lot to me."

"I get it," Maxwell said, backing away. "Your music is your passion."

Scarlet froze. "How do you know that?" she asked, wondering if the Wishling boy was truly just a Wishling.

"I heard you play, remember?"

Scarlet flashed back to the day before in the practice room. How long had Maxwell been standing there before he tapped her on the shoulder?

"Wait, that reminds me. I'm not going to let you go until you hear this new song I discovered." He took out his phone and gently handed over one of his earbuds. They sat down on the bench, and he played her what she thought was the most beautiful song she had ever heard.

"It's called 'Far Away,'" he told her. "It's got an awesome beat, right?"

She nodded. The song was about two people from two different worlds who had found each other through *destiny*. Something about the lyrics touched Scarlet. A light rain suddenly started to fall from the sky and the clouds grew increasingly gray. Maxwell quickly took back the earbud and put away his phone before the song ended. Just then, lightning struck and a downpour followed.

He shouted over the rain, "Let's get out of here!"

"Wait. You can't do that. The song didn't finish. How does it end? Do they stay together?" Scarlet shouted back to him.

"What?"

Scarlet shook her head, knowing it didn't matter how the song ended anyway. "Nothing," she whispered.

Maxwell wanted to know more about the mysterious girl. He asked, "Where do you have to be exactly, Scarlet? Is your mom picking you up?"

"Something like that," Scarlet replied, careful not to reveal too much.

"My sister, Holly, is picking me up today. I've got to go meet her at the center."

Scarlet caught herself glancing into Maxwell's green eyes, then shook herself out of the spell he had put her under, and shouted, "Right, your sister!" against the falling rain. She had gotten so caught up in getting to know the Wishling boy that she had lost track of the Wish Mission and hadn't learned a single new thing about Holly. She was no closer to figuring out what the bad wish was.

CHAPTER

Twelve

Clara strutted into rehearsal, completely trans-formed. A hush fell over the other students who sat in the audience waiting for Wordsworth to begin that day's rehearsal. Clara radiated a new confidence that set her apart from the others.

Whitney sat with her girl posse, admiring Clara's new look and attitude. "Are you seeing what I'm seeing?" Whitney asked them.

They all nodded in unison, jaws dropped.

Clara looked like Vivica's twin! They were both dressed in skinny jeans with strategically matching off-the-shoulder tops. Their hairstyles complemented each other, too. Vivica tied her platinum-blond hair back in a bun, carefully hiding her silvery-blue streak, while Clara's hair was pulled back in a tight ponytail. Both wore bright pink lip gloss and matching silver hoops in their ears.

"That intern has done amazing things for Clara's style," Nelle observed.

"Totally! I need to know what kind of lip gloss that is. It's unreal!" Whitney walked over to Clara to talk to her, but Clara didn't acknowledge her. Whitney quickly returned to her friends and sniffed, "Apparently, Clara has changed more than her look."

Behind the red curtain, the Star Darlings were dressed in all black, wearing tees and sweatpants, posing as stage crew. Rehearsal was about to begin, and Wordsworth stepped onto the stage. All eyes turned to him, including Vivica's and the Wisher's.

A former actor himself, the director boomed in a trained baritone voice, "Good afternoon. Rehearsal will begin shortly. The North Coast Arts Center's last show of the season—our all-star variety show—is just a few days away. I still haven't worked out the lineup, but we're going to run through all the acts today and see if this order works." He took a long dramatic pause. "Oh, yes, and I heard from the producer of *Song and Chance*, who confirmed she will be attending opening night. So go out there and put everything you have into these performances. This could be your big break!" Then he shouted with great enthusiasm, "Lights, curtains! Let's rehearse!"

As Clara headed down the aisle, lit only by teeny, tiny floor lights, she felt a chill run down her body. She was the first singing act in the show. A strong wind pushed her forward. She climbed the small set of stairs onto the stage and began her song.

For a moment, Sage and Leona forgot they were on Wishworld. Captivated by Clara's performance, they were struck by how talented she was and how much joy came from watching her perform. Her light, airy tone invited the audience to listen to every word she was singing. Her lyrics told a story of a little girl with big dreams. It was funny and sweet. But as Sage watched, she could see that Clara was holding back a bit, that she wasn't totally secure in her own talent.

Sage whispered to Leona, "How does Clara not see that she is such an amazing singer? What's missing here? Do you not see what I'm seeing?"

Scarlet interjected. "I see it."

Leona agreed. "She's missing what's right in front of her!"

Sage's eyes widened. "I've got it. Stopping Vivica from granting the Wisher's bad wish is only part of the mission. We also have to help show the Wisher how gifted she truly is!"

Sage's Star-Zap flashed. Her wish energy was dissipating, which meant that time was running out. The Star Darlings' pendants lit up, too, which told them they were getting closer to stopping the bad wish. They just needed to find a way to get through to the Wisher.

Sage thought, *If Vivica's powerful force field is stopping us from reaching Clara, then we have to find another way to get to her. We've got to show Clara that she has what it takes to be a star! But how?*

Clara's original song ended to loud applause from the other students in the audience.

Wordsworth smiled. "Nice job, Clara. Work on your projection so we can all hear you, and you'll be just fine for the show." Clara returned to her seat next to Vivica, hardly noticing the positive response she had received or Wordsworth's encouraging words. She saw only the negative, blocking out the applause, and was still convinced that no matter how good she sounded, Holly would always sound better and steal the show.

Clara grumbled, "*'Just fine'!* Wordsworth would never have said that to Holly. He would have told her how perfect she is and how she's the center's rising star."

Vivica smiled. Even though she still hadn't found a way to grant the young Wisher her bad wish yet, she knew the negatites were working and had overtaken Clara. Now it was time to guide Clara toward making her bad wish come true.

Wordsworth called Holly to the stage next. "Our shining star, Holly!" A music student started playing solo piano. Holly stepped into the spotlight and up to the microphone. She began to sing. After her first note floated through the air, the audience was silent.

Sage, Leona, and Scarlet turned their attention away from Vivica and Clara to listen to Holly's astounding voice.

Scarlet recognized the Wishling song. It was the love ballad Maxwell had played for her, "Far Away," but Holly had given it her own unique spin. The lyrics and the music were bringing Scarlet back to the time she had spent with Maxwell. She listened and felt something she had never felt before—like the space inside her chest was filled up with something almost painful, but she was really happy. Scarlet couldn't stop thinking about Maxwell, replaying certain moments, like when he had grabbed her hand to show her where to go, or when he had looked at her a certain way.

Sage watched as Scarlet's aura changed colors

from a saturated bright pink to a much softer pink. Even though Scarlet was on Wishworld, it was almost as if she was glowing. Something was going on with her. Sage wasn't sure, but she thought she even saw tears well in Scarlet's eyes. Sage lit up. "Oh, my stars! This Wishling love song is melting Scarlet's heart," she whispered to herself.

Leona tapped Sage on the shoulder and said, "Looks like the song is making Scarlet *feel* something!"

Neither girl had ever seen Scarlet react to anything that way before.

Sage turned to Scarlet and asked, "How do you know this song?"

Dreamy and distracted, Scarlet said, "Maxwell played it for me."

Scarlet must have feelings for Maxwell, Sage realized. And the music was bringing out the Starling's softer side.

Sage was suddenly distracted by a flash of blue light in the audience. She quickly shifted her attention from Scarlet to Clara, who was glaring at Holly onstage. A sizzling blue aura surrounded Clara now. It was invisible to a Wishling's eye, but Sage saw it.

Sage looked at Leona. "Can you hear any of what Vivica is saying to Clara?"

Leona tried out her special power of hearing from distances, but she still could not break through. She heard only loud static crackling.

Vivica leaned in closer to Clara. She really wanted to guide Clara to the bad wish. "*Soooo*, how long have you known Holly?" she asked.

Clara rolled her eyes. "I've known her since I was five. She's been my best friend ever since. Well, at least until now."

Vivica kept pushing. "Did she *always* hog the spotlight? I mean, look at her!"

As Clara watched Holly onstage, she thought about all the times Holly had gotten the lead in a performance or won the heart of a director or received a standing ovation. Vivica guided the conversation in hopes of gathering more details so that she could help grant Clara's bad wish as soon as possible.

Clara sighed. "I know. *I wish just one time I'd be able to outshine Holly!*"

Vivica felt a surge of negative energy fill her body. She tried to conceal her excitement at getting closer to granting the young Wisher's bad wish. She pictured Rancora on the Isle of Misera, proud of her Starling apprentice. It was only a matter of time before she would shine brighter than any of the Star Darlings on Starland!

Clara had spoken her bad wish, but that was only one part of the process. There was still the matter of timing the wish. A bad wish couldn't release its negative energy unless the timing was just right.

Anxious to get on with the wish granting, Vivica pried even more. "Or maybe the television producer who is coming to the performance would discover you instead of Holly?"

Clara looked at Vivica and thought about what she had just said. That idea had never crossed her mind. She didn't respond at first, but soon a smile appeared on her face. "That would be a dream come true! But it'll never happen as long as Holly is performing. I wish Holly would just disappear!"

Vivica studied Clara, searching for a clue. Then her teardrop necklace vibrated and crackled. A sharp blue light flashed from it. Negatites recharged her body. Vivica had an idea. *That's the wish! Holly needs to disappear!*

Holly finished her song. All the cast and crew in the theater stood up and clapped, even though it was only a rehearsal. Wordsworth turned to Holly before she stepped into the wings. "Perfection as usual, my young star. If you do what you did just then, you're going to impress the producer and land yourself a spot on television!" He clapped for her and then motioned to the whole cast, clapping for them, too. "Okay, let's carry on. We've only got another hour for this run-through, then dress rehearsal tomorrow and then . . . the show!"

The Star Darlings tried to track Vivica and Clara, but they were already gone. Vivica was still one step ahead of them.

The Star Darlings retreated to their storage room hideout to rest and regroup for the next step in the mission.

Sage sat in one corner of the cluttered room, trying to make sense of the mission. She wrote in her Cyber Journal. *Wishworld Observation #1: Latest development. At the variety show's rehearsal, the Wisher, Clara, was holding back when she performed her original song. If only Leona, Scarlet, and I could hold a mirror to her to show her how uniquely talented she truly is, maybe she could finally see it for herself and shine like the star she is. Maybe then she would stop comparing herself to Holly, and she wouldn't need to wish anything bad.*

In another corner of the room, Leona thought about how talented Clara and Holly were—and in such different ways. Seeing them both perform also reminded her that she hadn't sung a song since she'd landed on Wishworld. She missed that feeling of getting lost in the music. Watching the performers at rehearsal that day had inspired her. She knew she couldn't perform on Wishworld on that mission, but she still couldn't stop herself from wishing for it.

Scarlet stretched out on the old velvet love seat she had officially declared as her own. She needed a moment to herself, just like the other Star Darlings, to reflect on the mission so far. All she could think about was how all the holo-screens she had collected on her Star-Zap, and holo-projected throughout her dorm room on Starland, had not prepared her for that trip. Wishworld was more beautiful than she had remembered it. Would there ever be a time when a Starling could live on Wishworld and start a Wishling life there? Wishworld had captured her imagination and was maybe even stealing her heart.

CHAPTER
Thirteen

High in the sky above Wishworld, hidden behind a starry canvas of vibrant colors and shimmering starbursts, Lady Stella continued her late-night studies into Starland's ancient past at the Illumination Library. She pored over translucent scrolls and celestial artifacts, searching for answers to Starland's latest crisis. Since Rancora had been posing as Lady Cordial for some time, Lady Stella could not gauge just how much secret knowledge she had gathered and absorbed during her time at the academy.

She remembered with anger how much she had trusted "Lady Cordial," even taking her into her confidence and sharing with her the prophecy of the twelve Starlings who together would save Starland. Of course Rancora had used that information to hurt Starland even more.

But what Lady Stella was focusing on that night was the page of the oracle Rancora had taken when she was disguised as Lady Cordial. What information did it hold, and how was Rancora using it to her advantage?

The lights flickered throughout Starland, a reminder that some negative energy, enough to affect the balance of positive wish energy on Starland, had been released when Rancora intercepted the Bad Wish Orb. Lady Stella's Star-Zap flashed brightly. It was time for her to check the wish energy levels of the Star Darlings on Wishworld. She carefully studied the numbers. Sage, Leona, and Scarlet's collective wish energy had fallen to startlingly low levels, well below what any Starling had endured before while on a Wish Mission.

Lady Stella quickly made a cup of Zing and went back to her research. She couldn't stop thinking of Rancora. And as she held the warm cup in her hand, an image came to her so clearly that she knew it must mean something. It was Rancora, with her teardrop-shaped pendant. In a moment Lady Stella realized that Rancora must have given Vivica her pendant to collect the negative energy from the bad wish. She jumped up, spilling a bit of Zing on the table.

"The pendant. Of course!" she said. "The Star Darlings must take possession of the teardrop pendant if the mission is to succeed!"

Vega and Libby were fast asleep in their dorm rooms. Suddenly, they were awakened by their Star-Zaps.

Libby sat up in a flash. "Oh, my stars! What's happening?" She checked her Star-Zap. The message read URGENT, COME TO MY OFFICE AT ONCE! It was from Lady Stella.

Vega had already dressed and was out the door on her way to Lady Stella's office before Libby had even lifted her toothlight to brush her teeth. Vega immediately surmised that she would be going to Wishworld. Why else would Lady Stella call her to her office at that starhour? As she rushed down the Little Dipper Dormitory hallway, she wondered, *What has happened to Sage, Leona, and Scarlet? What has Vivica done? Is the mission in trouble?*

CHAPTER
Fourteen

DAY THREE

Two colorful streaks lit up the sky, one bright pink and the other a crystalline blue. On urgent instructions from Lady Stella, Libby and Vega were traveling down to Wishworld, on their way to deliver key information to Sage, Leona, and Scarlet: Vivica's teardrop pendant must be recovered at once. Vega and Libby had also brought reserves of the much-needed wish energy the Star Darlings needed to replenish their Wish Pendants.

When Vega and Libby showed up at the storage room, Sage was surprised and disheartened to see them. "What are you guys doing here?" she demanded. She was concerned Lady Stella had lost faith in her.

Libby motioned for Sage, Leona, and Scarlet to come to her so that she could recharge their pendants. As Libby restored the Wish Pendants to their full power, Vega explained, "There is new information we have to share with you guys!" She looked at the Star Darlings' Wish Pendants as she spoke. "Vivica's teardrop pendant. We have to get it from her!"

Alarmed, Sage said, "Our special powers aren't working on Vivica or her Wisher, Clara. We can't get through to Clara or even close to Vivica."

"That's what Lady Stella said—that as long as Vivica wears the pendant, she will be too powerful. If we take it from her, those powers will start to fade," added Libby, who had successfully recharged the Wish Pendants with positive wish energy.

Sage's eyes brightened at the new information. "Well, we've got more positive energy now.

Together, we can take the teardrop necklace!"

"Exactly!" Vega replied.

Sage looked at Scarlet, reflecting on how dreamy Scarlet had gotten when Holly sang the love ballad in rehearsal. She said with concern, "Scarlet, that means no distractions."

Scarlet jumped to her own defense. "I'm as focused as you and Leona," she retorted, although she knew deep down that Maxwell had sidetracked her. She didn't want to admit it to Sage or the other Star Darlings. As much as she was committed to the mission to save Starland, she found herself continually pushing down thoughts of Maxwell. Overwhelmed with emotion, Scarlet left the storage room in a huff. "I need to get out of here!"

Just then, an announcement came over the arts center speakers: *Dress rehearsal for the Spring Variety Show in the main theater is starting now!*

Leona leaped over to the hanging mirror. "This Wishling hair is way harder to manage than my hair on Starland. There's just no sparkle!"

"Leona, this isn't about your hair," Sage insisted. "We've got to get that teardrop pendant or the mission will fail."

Vega and Libby looked at each other. Libby leaned in to whisper to Vega: "Looks like we came at just the right time."

Everyone was energized by dress rehearsal jitters. It was the night before the big show—the last night of rehearsal. Sage and Leona, both dressed as stage crew, checked around the busy backstage area, crowded with students preparing for their acts. Some were listening to their headphones, tuning out the world, while others stretched in yoga positions or ran vocal scales to themselves.

Hiding in the wings of the theater, Sage looked around and whispered to Leona, "Where's Scarlet?"

"Don't see her anywhere," Leona said, searching to see if Scarlet was in the audience.

Scarlet had escaped to the girls' bathroom after she had stormed out of the storage room.

"The Star Darlings are right. I can't let down Starland over a Wishling boy!" She was alone, so she looked into the wide mirror above the sink. She wanted strength and focus before she spoke to Maxwell. She knew it was best to tell him she couldn't see him anymore. She recited her Mirror Mantra: "It's time for some star power!" A surge of positive energy filled her body. She hoped it would be enough to help her say good-bye to Maxwell and focus on the mission better.

As soon as she sent the Star-Zap message to Maxwell explaining that she was going to be too busy to hang out, she was surprised by a pang in her heart. She raced out of the girls' room, went back to the hideout to put on her stage crew clothes, and then quickly found Leona and Sage backstage.

"I'm back," she told them, out of breath. "Sorry about before. I'm all about the mission now, I promise."

"Then let's save Starland!" Sage said.

Wordsworth shouted to the Star Darlings, "Stage crew, out here now!" He saw Sage peeking out from the wings. "Hey, you!"

Sage pointed to herself. "Me?"

Scarlet reminded Sage and Leona, "We're *stage crew*!"

"Yes, you!" Wordsworth said impatiently.

Sage rushed into the audience, where the director was sitting. He looked at her. "I haven't seen you around here. Are you new?"

"Yes, I'm new. That's it. I'm new," Sage told the director.

"Of course, you're new," he said in agreement, and then got back to business. "We're working on the final lineup for the show. Bring this list to the assistant director."

"Absolutely." By the time she handed the list to the assistant director, Sage had already memorized the show order.

Then Wordsworth shouted, "Lights! I need a spotlight, yesterday!"

He saw Leona. "You. Stagehand. Over here! I need to check out the spotlight. Come here and stand center stage!" The director pointed right at her.

Leona flipped her wavy brown Wishling hair back and headed center stage under the spotlight, where she felt most at home. She loved the sensation of the warm light on her skin. For a moment, she imagined that she was back on Starland and asked, "Would you like me to sing for you, test out the microphone?"

Wordsworth barked, "Microphone? We're checking light cues, sweetheart. Auditions are over." Then he thought about it for a minute. "Wait, I have an idea. You know the show, right?"

Leona played along. "Of course!"

"Perfect. The dancers are off getting their final fittings, so I need some stand-ins to do the number for the lighting team. Why don't you show me some of the moves, okay?"

Leona hesitated at first. She tried to remember some of the dance moves she had learned on her first day on Wishworld, when she had joined the dance class. "A pirouette, right?" She smiled from ear to ear, hoping she had guessed the right move.

"This number is the modern dance. You do know that one, right?" he asked, running low on time and patience.

Leona pretended to know exactly what the director was talking about, and she nodded. "Yes, totally!" She looked at the wings and saw both Scarlet and Sage on their Star-Zaps, quickly looking up the definition of *modern dance*. She looked at them, shrugging.

The director pointed to Sage and Scarlet, too. "I'll need those two stagehands out onstage, as well."

Sage and Scarlet looked up, caught off guard. They walked onstage, with the spotlight following them.

Sage called out to the director, "Um, sorry, but we don't know the routine."

The director looked slightly annoyed but told her, "Just line up, listen to the music . . . and follow her lead." He pointed at Leona, then told them, "Do your best!"

Leona beamed. "I so have this one!" She immediately started dancing around the stage. The lighting team adjusted the lights, following Leona's interstellar moves around the stage.

Wordsworth grinned. He said sarcastically,

"How about we just start with the song first?"

Leona gasped. "Of course. Music!"

"Sound crew. Cue music!" Wordsworth shouted.

The music began. It was a high-energy beat, Leona's favorite. She did her best to remember the routine she had learned in dance class her first day there. With the spotlight on all three Star Darlings, they had no choice but to improvise the dance together. Leona slid across the stage, her friends trying to keep up with her, and she reminded them, "It's for the mission!"

The cast and crew turned to see what was happening onstage.

"Impressive for stage crew," Wordsworth called out to them. "Nice job. But I need one more volunteer. There are four dancers in this number." He waved to the sound team. "Stop the music!" He looked into the audience of students waiting to rehearse their acts. "Anyone want to volunteer?"

Someone called out, "I volunteer!"

The Star Darlings looked at each other. They

knew who that voice belonged to. It was a Starling, and her name was *Vivica*!

Vivica appeared from the audience, taking her time, dramatically making her way onto the stage. She was already dressed in dancewear, *almost like she had planned the whole thing.* Before the music started again, she noticed Vega and Libby standing in the wings. "You two are here, too? Three Star Darlings weren't enough for me?"

"Music!" shouted Wordsworth.

The Star Darlings began the dance again. Sage danced over to Leona and Scarlet. She told them, "We need the pendant! This is our chance!"

Wordsworth asked Vivica, "Are you ready?"

She answered with an air of complete confidence. "I've been ready for this for a very long time!" Her necklace crackled. She tucked it under her leotard.

Unbeknownst to the Wishlings who stood and watched the dance as the tech team adjusted sound and lights, this was a battle for a higher purpose, for the future of Starland!

Sage discovered that now that her energy levels were higher, her energy manipulation skills were more powerful. She concentrated on Vivica's necklace, visualizing the clasp in back and loosening it, while Scarlet tried with her special powers to throw Vivica off-balance and lift her off the ground. Leona moved around, ready to catch the teardrop necklace before it fell to the stage.

As Leona danced over to Vivica, Vivica grabbed Leona by the arm and pulled at her Wish Pendant cuff. She turned Leona around so fast that Leona lost her footing and slid across the stage.

The lighting crew tried desperately to keep up with all the action onstage. Wordsworth was enthralled. "What inspired movements! These girls are naturals!"

Leona checked herself out and appeared to be fine, but she was concerned that her cuff was damaged. She tried to reason with Vivica. "Why are you doing this to us?"

Sage effortlessly floated over to Vivica, who still seemed to be dancing for the lights. "Tell us what happened. Why are you helping Rancora?" Sage asked.

"You know why," Vivica insisted with great anger in her voice.

Scarlet leaped into the air in an attempt to look like she was dancing, but really she was trying to grab the teardrop necklace.

Vivica pointed at Scarlet and sent her flying into the air just as she was about to grab the necklace.

Scarlet, furious but more determined than ever to defeat Vivica, stood up and rejoined Sage and Leona. The Star Darlings formed a circle around Vivica, still modern-dancing their hearts out—or at least doing their best impression, based on the rehearsals they had watched.

"What are you talking about?" Leona asked. She truly didn't understand Vivica's fiery accusations.

"You and the Star Darlings have hurt me time and time again! You know exactly what you've done. I'm going to make sure it doesn't happen again!"

Sage shook her head. "We never did anything to you!"

"You make me feel invisible!" Vivica said.

"Everyone can shine on Starland. You know

that, Vivica!" Sage insisted. "Please give us the pendant." She reached out her hand. "For Starland!"

Vivica had been holding in her anger for so long she couldn't contain it anymore. "Starland? The Star Darlings do all the shining up on Starland. Starting with that whole band audition. That was a joke. Your band was chosen way before you sent out that flyer."

"Vivica, you're a Starling, just like us. Why would you want to work with Rancora to destroy Starland?" Leona asked.

"You're forgetting one thing: I'm not a Star Dipper, um, I mean, Star Darling." She felt a tinge of jealously whenever she said the words *Star Darlings*. Blue and black sparks shot out from her teardrop necklace. "I've stayed in the shadows too long. I'm sick of always being left out."

Sage knew the mission was on the line and tried to get through to Vivica. "You're as good as any of us."

Even though Leona had negative feelings toward Vivica, she felt herself letting go of her personal issues and tapping into the better part of herself that benefitted everyone on Starland. "Vivica, you're so talented. Your energy manipulation skills are amazing. No Starling can deny that."

"I'll never shine as brightly as the Star Darlings as long as Lady Stella is the headmistress at Starling Academy. Never! After I grant Clara's negative wish and release the Bad Wish Orb's negatites on Starland, Rancora's power will be restored. Then I'll be her only apprentice! I'll shine brighter than all the Star Darlings together! Imagine that!" She laughed in a mean-spirited way. Her necklace crackled and sparked again.

Sage watched in disbelief and thought about how angry Vivica had become since she had absorbed the negatites. She wanted to defend herself and the other Star Darlings but stopped. She suddenly knew why Vivica had turned against the Star Darlings and Starland.

Vivica had been hurt by them. They had not done it intentionally, but they had hurt her nevertheless. She had felt hidden in the shadows, invisible and ignored, just like the Wisher, Clara, felt. Sage finally understood that underneath Vivica's name-calling and snarky attitude, she really wanted to be a Star Darling. Vivica had felt left out when Lady Stella hadn't chosen her to be one of them, so she had turned to darkness, where she could receive all the attention she desired from Rancora, without any competition from the Star Darlings.

Sage tried to tap into the best part of Vivica and reach out to her that way. She assured her, "You don't have to do this!"

Scarlet urged Vivica, "Please stop your plans to grant Clara's bad wish."

"Starland needs a Starling like you," Leona said with open arms.

That startled Vivica. She was unsure how to react. She hadn't felt *seen* by the Star Darlings, and now there they were, acknowledging and praising her. She touched her teardrop necklace and reminded herself of her bad Wish Mission and the promise to Rancora. "You'll have a nice show tomorrow. I'm thinking of dedicating

Clara's performance to Starland. By the end of the show, the Star Darlings will lose their shine forever!"

"End of the show?" Sage asked Vivica, looking at the other Star Darlings. Could that be when the bad wish would be granted?

Just as Vivica was about to respond, Wordsworth stopped the dance. "We've got the light cues set now and the sound levels, too. Thank you, girls. Nice intensity to the dancing. You should consider auditioning next season. I like your commitment."

Vivica smirked, pointing to Leona's Wish Pendant cuff. "Did you break something?"

Leona covered her pendant with one hand, then checked it. It appeared to be okay. She'd have to take a closer look later.

Vivica strutted offstage and left a trail of fiery blue and black sparks in her path as she exited the theater. She imagined that Rancora was exceedingly pleased with her progress on the mission. In one more day, the bad wish would be granted!

Oblivious to the extreme tension between the Star Darlings and Vivica, Wordsworth turned to the cast and crew. "Dress rehearsal is over. Tomorrow is showtime, everyone! Get some rest. Except stage crew." He looked at the Star Darlings. "I need this theater cleaned up and prepped for tomorrow. Now! Got it?"

Exhausted, the Star Darlings nodded at Wordsworth. They had just experienced a major setback on the mission and had failed to gain control of the powerful teardrop pendant. Sage smiled weakly. "We're on it! The theater will be ready for opening night."

The question was, would the Star Darlings be ready?

CHAPTER
Fifteen

After everyone left the theater, the Star Darlings started prepping for opening night. Sage and Leona wheeled the backdrop scenery offstage and put away props while Libby and Vega hung the costumes and straightened the makeup trays for the big show.

Sage looked at Scarlet, who had taken a seat at a drum set that was in the band pit. Scarlet flipped on her Star-Zap, took out her Starland drumsticks, and started drumming softly to a song.

Sage was unaware that Scarlet was listening to "Far Away," the song Maxwell had played for her, and Holly had sung at rehearsal. Something sparked inside Scarlet when she listened to it. *Inspiration!* She turned up the volume and discovered an amazing new drum rhythm. She was fully immersed in the music, adding her own touch to the song.

After she had been playing for a few minutes, Scarlet looked up from the drums at the Star Darlings, who had gathered around her. She stopped drumming and confessed to them, "I've never felt this way before. From the moment I met Maxwell, I've been getting these strange symptoms."

"Like what?" Sage asked.

"There's a warm feeling in my heart. I'm forgetful. I'm losing track of time, and I can't seem to stop thinking about him."

Sage began to piece it together. "Wait, a warm feeling in your heart, losing track of time . . ."

"Daydreaming about a boy?" Leona asked. She looked at Sage. "Is that *our Scarlet*?"

Sage looked at Scarlet. "I saw the way your aura glowed when Holly sang that love song. I watched you transform. . . . Oh, my stars, you have a *crush* on a boy! And he's a Wishling!"

The rest of the Star Darlings squealed in excitement.

Scarlet was quick to deny it. "Of course not! It's about Wishworld. I'm starstruck by this place."

"It's not about Wishworld, Scarlet," Sage said.

Scarlet was about to say something, then stopped herself. Sage was right! It *was* about Maxwell. Scarlet didn't want to admit it, but she couldn't deny it, either. Embarrassed and unaccustomed to the feelings she was having, Scarlet bowed her head. The other Star Darlings circled her with sparkling enthusiasm. They were beyond stoked for Scarlet.

Leona announced, *"Scarlet is having a feeling!"*

Something sparked inside Scarlet. She cracked a smile. Her aura glowed. A creative display of glistening stardust burst into the air. Scarlet picked up her drumsticks and started playing again. She felt happy and free. Her drum combinations were fresh and imaginative, way more inventive than any time she'd ever played on

Starland. She took a deep breath and tried the drum trick she had failed to master during the practice sessions for the Light Giving Day performance. She closed her eyes, thought about the feelings she had for Maxwell, and let those feelings guide her through the music. It worked! She performed the drum trick perfectly. Powered by a true and positive feeling for someone else, Scarlet expressed herself through her music and found her groove again!

Inspired, Vega picked up the electric bass that had been sitting in its stand, just waiting for her. She started to jam along with Scarlet. Libby sat down at the keyboards and began to play along, too. Sage picked up the guitar from the stand and strapped it on. She found the notes to complete the melody. Leona tried singing, but her voice was noticeably weak. She started playing tambourine instead of pushing her voice any further.

Led by Scarlet's incredible beat, the Star Darlings jammed together.

Sage looked at Scarlet, who was clearly more inspired and openhearted than she'd ever known her to be before. Sage told her, "When Holly sang the song he had played for you, it sparked something in you. The music helped you realize your true feelings for him."

As soon as Sage heard herself say that, she knew she had hit on something important. Music had the power to change people's hearts. The right song, played at the right time, could have a truly powerful effect on someone. And maybe, just maybe, *that* was the way to get through to Clara. Sage felt as though she had discovered the key to saving Starland. A surge of wish energy flowed throughout her body. Her Wish Pendant necklace lit up, confirming it. She stopped playing guitar and shared her idea with her friends.

"I just had this thought. It might be crazy, but maybe music can change Clara's bad wish to a good wish?" Sage told her friends.

"I'm not sure I get it," Vega said, confused.

"You know that feeling you get when you listen to a song that, like, *speaks* to you?" Sage asked. "Like there's something about the music and the lyrics that gets at your heart, makes you feel something really strongly?"

All the girls nodded.

"Like when a song makes you cry, but in a good way!" Libby exclaimed.

"Or makes you feel invincible," Leona said.

"Or makes you feel understood, like someone gets you," Scarlet added softly.

"Yes!" Sage replied. "Music can be powerful. If we find the right music and the right lyrics that Clara will connect with, it might just be the key to turning Clara's wish around. Maybe this mission can be a success after all."

"Well, it's worth a try," Scarlet said. "Nothing else has worked."

Not missing a beat, Scarlet busted out a drum solo, then enthusiastically suggested to the girls, "Let's write a song!"

"Yes, a song. Star Darlings, we're going to write a song!" Sage strummed the guitar.

Leona asked with a hoarse voice, "Could this song actually save Starland?"

Sage turned to her. "You okay?"

"Just didn't warm up my voice, that's all." Leona coughed a few times and began her warm-ups, although she soon discovered that her voice was cracking and warbly. She began to get worried.

Sage turned to the Star Darlings band. "How about we all warm up now!" She was certain they were on the right track. "We'll write a song to save Starland and help Clara connect with her better self. Then she'll see how she can shine on her own!"

"She's spent too long in the shadows!" Leona whispered, saving her voice for the singing.

Sage's eyes lit up. "Yes! That's what Vivica said to us. And I think that's how Clara feels about Holly. . . . I know, let's use those words in the song!"

"But Holly never tried to keep Clara in the shadows," Leona insisted.

"It doesn't matter. That's how Clara felt," Sage explained.

"Especially when Clara's mind was just clouded by negative thoughts!" Scarlet added, tightening the drumhead and getting ready to play again.

Sage lifted her hands in the air. "Star Darlings,

our song is going to inspire the Wisher, Clara, to see how amazing she truly is and show her that she's a *shining star*! That she doesn't need to dim Holly's glow for her own to shine!"

The Star Darlings got down to the business of creating a song that would touch Clara's heart. They stayed up all night, writing and playing music, snacking on treats, and jamming. As they wrote the song, sparkles of every color, including crimson, gold, lavender, pink, and blue, shined brightly throughout the theater. Sweet music filled the air. It was so lovely and melodic it might have even reached Starland.

Late that night, under a full moon, while the other Star Darlings slept, Sage sat with her Cyber Journal. She was excited to report her wish-changing observation. *Wishworld Observation #2: Vivica's powers are strong, and we were not able to get the teardrop pendant off her. But today we discovered that music possesses healing and transformative powers! Of course, there are still*

many unanswered questions. What we do know from Vivica is that the bad wish will be granted by the end of the Spring Variety Show, but we don't know the full extent of Vivica's plan or how and when she will guide Clara to fulfill her bad wish.

Sage looked up from her Cyber Journal. She read aloud something she had just written: " 'The bad wish will be granted by the end of the Spring Variety Show.' "

She stood up and woke the others, announcing, "We've got to play our song before the show ends." She gasped. "Intermission! That's it. Yes! Then maybe we'll have a chance to change Clara's wish when she hears our new song."

CHAPTER

Sixteen

Sage thought about the song the Star Darlings band had created the night before and felt hopeful, but she knew that Vivica's negatite-powered wish energy would be a challenge for them. She hoped that the power of the song would change all that. The plan was to use her power of persuasion over Wishling adults to convince Wordsworth to include the Star Darlings in the lineup, and they would entertain the audience during intermission. If all went well, Clara would hear the song and it would inspire a change of heart in her. It was their only hope of turning her bad wish to a good wish. Sage was relying on her intuition that it would work.

For added strength, Sage looked into the mirror in the backstage dressing room and recited her Mirror Mantra: *"I believe in you. Glow for it!"* She needed an extra boost to face her last test for the Wish Mission. The Star Darlings' song at intermission just had to work!

Leona sat in the audience to keep an eye on Vivica while Sage covered the wings of the stage, helping with set changes and ensuring that Holly was never too far out of her sight. Leona knew the success or failure of the mission would be decided that night, and she wanted to do her part. She took out a compact mirror she had found in the dressing room, and repeated to herself, *"You are a star. Light up the world!"*

After reciting her Mirror Mantra that time, Leona felt more illuminated, but still her positive wish energy was not at its full star power. She lifted her sleeve to check her Wish Pendant cuff and discovered a small crack in it. Her pendant had been damaged, something she had feared. That explained her weakened voice. "What do I do? Tell the Star Darlings? I'd better keep it quiet for now. No distractions!"

In the back of the audience, Scarlet watched from another vantage point for any unusual moves made by Holly, Clara, or Vivica. Instead of finding the three girls, she spotted Maxwell. She didn't know the Wishworld customs for handling awkward moments between girls and boys. Was she supposed to run up to him and say hello first, or was he supposed to do that? Should she mention that she felt bad about telling him she couldn't see him anymore without any real explanation, or should she not say anything at all? If only she had studied harder in Wishworld Relations class! She looked at the wall clock and saw that she had enough time to quickly run to the girls' room to recite her Mirror Mantra. She needed the extra boost to successfully complete the mission. On the way to the girls' room, she whispered her mantra: *"It's time for some star power!"*

Backstage, opening night chaos was in full swing. There was extra tension in the air, too, since someone had just spotted the television producer from *Song and Chance* in the lobby. Cast members rushed around in different directions. Some performers chose to practice scales at the last minute. Others frantically adjusted their costumes and meticulously applied makeup, while a few sat against the wall, listening to their favorite tunes on their headphones to clear their minds before the big show.

Libby and Vega were covering the dressing room. They posed as hair-and-makeup assistants. They both kept a lookout for Clara and Holly, but so far there was no sign of either of them.

In the dressing room, a young Wishling shouted to Libby, "Hair spray, please. Extra hold!"

Libby looked at Vega, who just shrugged. "I know I studied what hair spray was, but now I can't seem to find any here." Libby used her gift of transforming objects to turn a hairbrush that had been sitting on the table into a bottle of extra-hold hair spray.

"I'm never going to be ready for the show at this rate," insisted the Wishling, staring at herself in the mirror with black netting in her hair and bright red lipstick on her lips.

"Hair spray coming your way," said Libby cheerfully, passing the hair spray down the line of girls who sat in front of a long mirror lit with oversized lightbulbs that shone blindingly.

Next another Wishling shouted to Libby, "Hairbrush, please!"

"Starf!" Libby had just transformed the hairbrush into a bottle of hair spray! Libby semi-panicked while she looked around the long makeup table for an object to transform into a hairbrush. *Now what?* she wondered.

Meanwhile, Vega rolled a costume cart behind Libby. She whispered to Libby, "Where's Clara?

I've lost track of her. I can't find her anywhere."

"I have no idea," Libby said. Then she asked, "Did you happen to see a hairbrush?"

"Moonbeams, Libby. We're on a mission to save Starland, and all you can think about is what your hair looks like?" Vega took a step back to check out Libby, whose long hair had turned a light brown with a single pink wave. "You could pull back the bangs a little. Otherwise, you look great."

Libby giggled. "Not for me, Vega. The hairbrush is for—"

The Star Darlings heard another shout from the young Wishling student performer impatiently waiting for a hairbrush. "Have you found the hairbrush? I'm on in ten minutes!"

Libby pointed to the Wishling girl. "Her!" She giggled again.

Vega used her mind control to make sure the Wishling was happy with her hair as it was and no longer needed a hairbrush. "Done! The situation is under control. Now, I've got to find Clara!"

The Wishling who had demanded the

hairbrush now said politely to Libby, "No need for a hairbrush. I actually think my hair looks fantastic just the way it is!"

Vivica and Clara were at the far side of the arts center building, out of sight of the cast and crew. Vivica assured Clara, "It's all set. I have a plan to make Holly disappear so the producer won't have a chance to see her."

Clara looked around the dark hallway, far from backstage. "Shouldn't we get back? I'm up first, and it's kind of a big night for me."

The lights flickered in the hallway. That meant the show was only minutes from starting.

Vivica's mood suddenly shifted. She found it hard to contain her frustration with the Wishling. Time was running out for her to grant her bad wish. The Star Darlings were closing in, and Rancora was most certainly weakening with every starmin that passed. Didn't Clara know how hard Vivica was working to grant her wish for her? What an ungrateful Wishling! Vivica mumbled, "You don't think I know this is a big night for you? It's an ever bigger night for me!"

Clara backed away. "What are you saying? You're not in the show. I am!" Vivica's teardrop necklace crackled. Clara felt a chill fall over her. "What's happened to you? I thought you were my friend."

Vivica was on edge. She needed the bad wish to be granted as much as the Star Darlings needed it to be stopped. So much was at stake. If she failed, Rancora would never trust her again. Since Vivica had turned her back on Lady Stella and Starland, there was nothing left for her at Starling Academy. She didn't know what she would do if she didn't come through for Rancora. Vivica needed to maintain the trust of the Wisher if her plan was to succeed. She took a deep breath and smiled, reminding herself, *By curtain call tonight, Clara's wish will be granted, and Rancora will reward me.*

Softly, she said to Clara, "This is *your wish*!" She pointed to a closed door with a sign on it that read PROPS.

Clara anxiously looked at the wall clock. "Props? I don't need any props. I've really got to get onstage," she insisted. She walked away from Vivica, heading toward the theater.

Vivica held out her finger and created a strong energy force that stopped Clara in her tracks. Under Vivica's control, Clara turned to her. Vivica opened the door and turned on the light, revealing a small empty prop room. "This is where Holly will be hanging out during the show. Away from the lights and noise. Where no one can hear her."

Vivica used the power of the negative energy left in the pendant to persuade Clara to follow her plan without questioning it. Clara stood frozen, just staring at Vivica, as Vivica instructed her, "After you perform your song, you'll reach out to Holly as a friend. Tell her you missed her. Ask her if she would take a quick walk with you."

Entranced by Vivica, Clara nodded. "Finish my song. Tell Holly I miss her. Ask Holly to take a walk."

"Tell her there's a prop that Wordsworth asked you to retrieve for one of the performers. She'll agree. Then bring her here," Vivica continued, pointing to the prop closet. "Close the door. It will lock automatically. I've got the only key, so there'll be no problem there. Then—*poof!*—no more Holly. If the producer can't see her perform, there will be no one to steal your thunder. You'll finally get to be the star."

Perplexed at first, Clara stared at Vivica, but then a smile moved across her face. "Of course. Holly will disappear!"

"Like magic!" Vivica said, knowing that her plan would work and that the bad wish would be granted before the Star Darlings could stop her.

Backstage, Sage tracked Holly's every move. She watched as Holly stood in the wings, all made up, radiant, ready to sing for the producer. She could tell that Holly had opening-night nerves. Sage walked over to her.

"Good luck tonight, Holly!" Sage chirped.

"Thank you," Holly replied warmly.

"I know you're gonna be great," Sage said enthusiastically.

Holly smiled at Sage, then snuck a peek from the wings into the audience. She saw the television producer who was scouting new talent for *Song and Chance* slip in through the back door and slide discreetly into the seat Wordsworth had reserved for her. The producer looked unhappy and checked her phone multiple times.

Holly whispered excitedly to Sage, "The *Song and Chance* producer is here!"

Meanwhile, Leona had lost track of Clara. She searched for her backstage. When she didn't find her, she holo-texted the other Star Darlings to check if they had seen her leave the theater.

The lights flickered again. The director spoke to the backstage cast and crew in a hushed voice. "Take your places, please."

Clara appeared just in time to take her place on the stage. Sage spotted her and quickly Star-Zapped the others to confirm Clara was back in view. THE WISHER IS HERE. IT'S SHOWTIME! KEEP

YOUR EYES OPEN FOR ANY UNUSUAL MOVEMENT, AND KEEP THE WISHER IN YOUR SIGHT AT ALL TIMES! GOOD LUCK, STAR DARLINGS! WE CAN DO THIS THING!

The lights dimmed. Music rose from the pit band. The audience settled into their seats. The red velvet curtains opened, revealing an empty stage.

Clara walked onstage from the wings to a round of applause. She wore a headband in her hair and was dressed in a flowered sundress and knee-high leather boots. She looked beautiful and glowed inside and out. Clara thought about what she was planning to do to Holly, but before she could have a second thought about it, Vivica peered at her from offstage, invisibly commanding Clara to look toward her. Clara turned her head. Vivica stared into her eyes and whispered, just loudly enough for her, but not the audience, to hear, "Holly won't steal your spotlight now. Tonight is your turn to shine!"

Clara nodded, then turned back to the audience. She bowed her head and spoke into the mic in a breathy, shaky voice. "I wrote this song one day when I realized how much music meant to me. Kind of, well, pretty much everything. I hope you enjoy it."

Within a few notes, Clara had captured the television producer's full attention. She performed with a playful and natural ease she'd been carrying inside but had never let shine through. That was her chance and she was taking full advantage of it. The producer leaned forward whenever Clara's lyrics stirred a reaction in the audience. Her pitch was perfect. Her style and tone were all her own.

The Star Darlings, anxious to get onstage, counted the minutes until they could perform at intermission. Even though they weren't sure exactly how the bad wish would play out, they knew that at any starmin it could be granted, and they were poised to stop it. They also knew they needed to keep a close watch on both Clara and Holly.

After Clara's stellar performance, the audience gave her a standing ovation. She was glowing as she walked offstage.

Sage told Leona, "You and the others follow

Clara. I'm watching Holly." But when she looked at where Holly had just been standing, she gasped. "Wait, I don't see her now!"

Suddenly, Vivica swooped in and tapped Sage on the shoulder. She smiled and asked, "Enjoying the show?"

Sage started to answer but thought better of it.

Then Vivica said menacingly, "There's more to come. You'll see. It just gets better." With that, she turned around and disappeared into the audience.

The next act began before the Star Darlings could dash after Clara, and they were stuck backstage. Wordsworth gestured to them. "Stage crew! Back it up! There's a performance going on. Quiet!"

Clara finally found Holly. She was all by herself in a hidden part of backstage, softly practicing her song. She looked nervous and unsure of herself. Clara moved right in and said in a warm, friendly voice, "Hi."

Holly looked around to see if Clara was talking to someone else.

Clara laughed. "I'm talking to you." She looked into Holly's eyes. "I'm sorry for the way I've been acting."

Holly melted. She couldn't believe what she was hearing. All her nerves for her performance started to float away.

"Will you forgive me?" Clara asked.

Holly looked relieved. "Yes, but what happened?"

"It's complicated," Clara said. "Can we go somewhere and talk for a minute?"

Holly nodded. "Yeah, but it'll have to be quick. I'm up soon."

"Don't worry about it," Clara said sweetly. Then she grabbed Holly's hand and guided her away from the theater and down the hall toward the prop closet.

The Spring Variety Show was a hit! Even the television producer seemed to be enjoying it. Although her poker face didn't reveal too much, at least she was still there! Wordsworth watched proudly. He was particularly impressed with Clara's song and suspected that she might have a chance at a spot in the singing competition.

It was time for Holly to perform. Wordsworth proudly announced, "Next up, one of our rising young stars at North Coast Performing Arts Center . . . I am extremely pleased to present . . . Holly!"

The piano player began the introduction to Holly's song, but Holly didn't walk onstage on her cue.

Vivica was lurking in a dark corner backstage. Clara found her and rushed up to her, out of breath.

"I did it," she whispered.

"Well done," Vivica said, and her teardrop pendant crackled.

The Star Darlings were in the wings, sitting in a circle, holding their instruments.

Sage reminded the others, "We go on right after Holly."

Scarlet asked, "What if the song doesn't work?"

"It's going to work," Leona said.

"As long as we work together, we have a chance," Sage said. She realized at that moment that she couldn't complete the mission without the help of *all* the Star Darlings who were there. They were *all* needed to play a song for the Wisher.

Vega calculated in her mind. "We have approximately seven Wishling minutes until we find out if the song will have an effect on Clara or not."

Suddenly, the assistant director ran over to the Star Darlings. Out of breath, she asked frantically, "Have you seen Holly? No one can find her anywhere!"

"What are you talking about?" Sage asked.

"She's supposed to be onstage now! But nobody knows where she is," she explained before rushing off to look elsewhere.

Sage looked at the other Star Darlings. *"Vivica!"* she exclaimed. "The bad wish has started!"

Wordsworth stood offstage, unable to utter even a single word. He stared in disbelief, shocked that the arts center's shining star, Holly, had abandoned the show at the last minute. He stalled for a moment. Then Sage raced up to him, wearing her electric guitar. "We can play now!"

CHAPTER

Seventeen

Wordsworth announced in his booming voice, "There's been a change in the show's lineup. Next up, some new talent. Ladies and gentlemen, please put your hands together for five of our bright stars. The . . ." He had momentarily forgotten the name of the band.

The audience was silent, looking at the five girls.

Sage helped him out. With full force, she shouted, "We're the *Star Darlings*. And this is our song. We call it 'When We Shine'!"

She sent out a wish of her own: for the

celestial positive energy of their song to reverse the negative feelings in Clara's heart and stop the bad wish.

Vivica, who had been lurking at the back of the theater, looked on in disbelief and annoyance. "The Star Dippers?" she muttered to herself.

Sage turned to the Star Darlings band members. They were tuned up and ready to save Starland! Leona was at the microphone; Vega was on the bass; Libby was at the keytar; and Scarlet was at the drums. Sage strummed the first note on her lead guitar. Then Scarlet counted out the beat: "And one, two, one, two, three, four!" As soon as the Star Darlings began their song, the audience got on their feet.

Leona's voice was still weakened from the damaged Wish Pendant, so Sage backed her up. Together, they sang.

If you've stayed too long in the shadows
Always the lonely one
If you're feeling left out, feeling less than
You're not the only one.

Vivica's teardrop necklace crackled and then sputtered. "What are they up to? Why are they playing this song?"

Backstage, Clara heard the audience cheering. She knew it wasn't Holly they were cheering for, and she wondered who was out there.

The assistant director rushed by her. Clara stopped her and asked, "What's happening out there?"

"Holly didn't show, so there's a girl band playing instead . . . and they're killing it!"

"Girl band? They weren't in the lineup." She followed the other cast and crew, who were all rushing to the side of the stage to check out the band. Clara saw the Star Darlings, and as she listened for a second, the song caught her attention. She moved closer to the stage to listen to the lyrics.

If you've ever wanted something so bad
And you feel overlooked
Jealous over what you don't have
There's another way, take a second look

Something in her shifted. She felt like her chest had been cracked open. She felt understood and sad and alive, all at the same time. When Sage and Leona sang the chorus, Clara realized she was crying.

Step into the sunlight
You and I
It's our sky
And we were meant to be
Sunlight burning bright
Look up, look up now
Together we can light the spark
Dynamite taking out the dark . . .

Clara leaned back against the wall and slumped down. She brought her forehead to her knees and let the tears fall freely down her cheeks. Those lines in the chorus hit a note in her: *"Step into the sunlight. You and I, it's our sky."* It made her long for Holly and their friendship. As the song played, it was truly magical.

She remembered what it had been like when she and Holly were on the same team. All the negativity she had been feeling left her body.

Clara was overcome with a realization—that Holly wasn't keeping her in the shadows. If anything, her own jealousy was. At that moment Clara knew the only thing really holding her back was herself. Why had she been comparing herself to Holly? Couldn't they both be amazing in their own unique ways? There was room for both of them to shine!

Meanwhile, Vivica frantically tried to stop the Star Darlings from finishing their song. She realized the words *too long in the shadows* were basically her own. She shouted to the audience, "The Star Dippers stole my words!" But nobody even noticed her. She had absolutely no effect on them. They were too busy dancing to the Star Darlings' music.

Vivica stormed down the aisle. The memories she had stored of all the times the Star Darlings had outshined her at Starling Academy flashed before her. And now this—when the bad wish was about to come true! Vivica knew that as long as the show was under way, there was still a chance for Holly to return, and then the bad wish wouldn't be granted by curtain call. And if that happened, it would mean, once again, that the Star Darlings had one-upped her. This was only intermission; there was more time for Holly to perform. Vivica screamed, *"Clara!"*

But Clara was already pushing through the crowd, trying to get to her friend. She wanted to get Holly out of that room and back onstage, where she belonged. She wanted the TV producer to hear Holly sing. She had turned her bad wish into a good one, but was it too late?

Just then, Leona's super hearing returned. Libby was doing a mini keytar solo, so Leona wasn't singing for a moment, and that was when she picked up something disturbing. She said to Sage and Scarlet, "I hear someone!"

As Libby played on, Sage mouthed, "Who?"

Leona closed her eyes and listened. She heard, *"Help! I'm stuck in here! The lock isn't working. I need to get out! Help!"* Leona opened her eyes and turned to Scarlet. "Oh, my stars! It's Holly! She's locked in a room somewhere in the building."

Scarlet stuck her drumsticks in her back pocket and told her friends, "Keep playing, I'll find her."

Leona nodded toward where she had heard the screams. "That way!"

Scarlet snuck offstage, and as Libby ended her keytar solo, Sage kept the song going, handing Leona a tambourine to keep the beat, since Scarlet wasn't there.

Sage told Leona, Vega, and Libby, "Keep singing, no matter what. *The song is working!* I can feel it!"

෩

Before Vivica could stop her, Clara headed straight to the prop room, which was down a long hallway, away from where anyone would be going that night. She could hear Holly's screams as she got closer. When she got there, she was surprised to see Scarlet there, about to pull the door open. Embarrassed, Clara looked at Scarlet.

Scarlet gave Clara a small smile and opened the door.

Holly practically fell into the hallway, and

Clara grabbed her best friend. "Come on, let's go!" she said, pulling Holly down the hall toward the theater.

Holly was out of breath and exhausted, but overjoyed to see Clara. "I'm so glad you're here. Thanks for finding help." She turned and gave Scarlet a grateful smile, thinking she had done something special to open the door.

"Yeah, um . . . we'll talk about it later," Clara replied. She looked at Holly with a mixture of guilt and relief. "Now we've got to get you to the stage. You've got a song to sing!"

"A song to sing!" Scarlet repeated. "Starf! I've got to get back onstage." She raced ahead of the girls, down the hallway to the stage, and then slid back into the seat at her drums and started drumming again.

The Star Darlings sang, and Sage looked right at Vivica and smiled. She meant it. Writing the song had allowed her to understand how hurt and jealous Vivica felt. At that moment, the song began to crescendo. It was powerful; Vivica caught herself singing along. She noticed that her negative feelings were dissipating the longer the

Star Darlings played their song, like it had some kind of magic. When she touched the teardrop necklace, it no longer crackled and shook. She knew that the song had something to do with the bad wish's not being granted. Strangely, her anger toward the Star Darlings started to fade. She didn't know what had come over her, but she felt less angry. She felt good. She felt hopeful.

The music brought Vivica back to when she'd first arrived at Starling Academy, as a young Starling with great possibilities and her own dream of expressing herself through singing and music. As Vivica remembered that, the negativity continued to lose its power over her, just as Leona's voice started to regain its full power!

Sage, who was still watching Vivica, saw her icy-blue aura brighten just like Scarlet's aura had brightened when she was feeling something for Maxwell. When the Star Darlings finished their song, Sage noticed Vivica clapping along with the audience. She hadn't imagined the song's positively affecting Vivica in that way. That hadn't been in the plan! They had written it for Clara, but of course Vivica had connected to it as well.

It made perfect sense! Watching how the power of music transformed even Vivica, Sage knew that she had discovered something important.

Wordsworth was about to announce the next act when Sage saw Clara and Holly in the wings. Sage rushed up to the microphone and whispered something in Wordsworth's ear. He stepped away. Sage waved Clara and Holly onto the stage. Clara reached for Holly's hand. Together they walked up to the mic.

Clara began, "Everyone, you have no idea how happy and thrilled I am to introduce my best friend ever. She is the most talented singer I know, and the truest friend, too . . . Holly!"

Since there was no piano onstage anymore, Holly asked if the Star Darlings band could back her up. Then she stepped up and took her place center stage. She sang the love ballad "Far Away" with such conviction and beauty even the television producer was visibly moved. Holly's voice touched everyone in the room.

After the song, while Holly took her bow, Clara stood with the Star Darlings. Now there was no invisible wall between them. She thanked

Scarlet for helping Holly, unaware that all the Star Darlings in each of their unique ways had helped her, too. Then she told the Star Darlings, "It might sound silly, but tonight feels really magical."

Sage looked at Clara. "You know what? It doesn't sound silly at all."

CHAPTER

Eighteen

At curtain call, Holly and Clara bowed in a line with the rest of the variety show's cast and crew. The audience members were on their feet, clapping and cheering.

"There's something I should tell you, Holly," Clara said. "Your getting locked in the closet wasn't exactly an accident, I planned it. I was jealous. And I'm so ashamed and sorry I did it. I understand if you never forgive me."

Holly took in that information. Clara waited, expecting the worst. She knew what she'd done was awful. After a long beat, Holly finally responded.

"It's okay," she said.

"What? You don't hate me?" Clara asked, shocked.

"No. Because you came back to get me. You didn't let the bad thing happen."

Clara gave her friend a fierce hug. She felt really lucky.

"I just don't want to let anything get in the way of our friendship ever again!" Holly said.

"Me neither!" Clara told her.

Backstage, there was much to celebrate!

Clara and Holly were inseparable, laughing and giggling together, making up for the last few weeks when they hadn't spoken or spent time together.

Wordsworth clinked a water glass and asked for everyone's attention. "To the cast and crew of North Coast Performing Arts Center!" Cheers broke out. "Kids, I'm proud of all of you. Tonight, all the performers onstage and the backstage crew proved why you've earned your spot at one of the most prestigious performance houses in the Northwest." He looked at Holly. "Holly, you sang beautifully, as usual." He then pointed to Clara and smiled. "Ladies and gentlemen, a new star was born tonight! I see big things for you in the future, Clara!" The cast and crew all clapped for her.

Wordsworth walked over to Clara and told her, "Clara, I always knew you were special. That's why you were here at the performing arts center. But today, you proved it to yourself! Congratulations!"

Holly turned to Clara and asked, "By the way, why didn't you ever tell me you wanted center stage?"

"I thought it was obvious."

"It wasn't!" Holly looked at her friend with tears in her eyes. "I am so happy that you had your moment today, Clara. I'm even happier to have my best friend back!"

Just then, the television producer arrived backstage. The cast and crew cleared the way for her as she made a beeline for Holly. She excitedly shook Holly's hand and introduced herself.

"Well, Holly," she said, "that was a powerful performance. You clearly know your way around a ballad. I know the show's viewers will love you. How would you like to audition for our show?"

Holly blushed. "I mean . . ."

Clara answered for her. "She'll do it!"

The woman smiled. Clara was genuinely thrilled for Holly and gave her a huge hug. The producer then reached out her hand to Clara. "And you, girl—you are an original! I haven't heard a sound quite like yours before. Would you consider auditioning for the show, too?"

Clara was shocked and beyond thrilled. "Yes, of course!" she exclaimed.

Holly grabbed her hand and squeezed it. "I knew you would get a spot," she told Clara, her eyes filled with happiness at the news that the amazing opportunity was happening for both of them.

The producer observed, "I have to say, I love when friends support each other. It's one of my favorite things to see."

But what the producer couldn't see, and what was even more beautiful, was the massive amount of exquisite positive wish energy pouring out of Clara and into Sage's, Leona's, and Scarlet's Wish Pendants. The wish energy was extra special because it came from Clara's understanding of how special she truly was, and her realization that she didn't have to bring someone else down to lift herself up.

The Star Darlings loved watching the happiness of the Wisher and her friend. They wished they could stay longer and spend more time with Clara and Holly now that the two were close again. But they had to move quickly. They needed to say their good-byes and return to Starland in order to deliver as much positive wish energy as possible.

Sage turned to the other Star Darlings. She told them, "Vivica already left for Starland. I saw her sneak off during Wordsworth's speech."

"Do you think Lady Stella will expel her?" Scarlet asked.

"Who knows? Vivica was overtaken by negative energy and was under Rancora's control . . . until we changed all that!" Leona said.

"Anyway, it's time for us to say good-bye to our Wishling friends," Sage reminded them.

The Star Darlings approached Clara and Holly. Clara couldn't contain her excitement. "Holly and I were chosen to audition for *Song and Chance*. It's going to be on TV! You have to promise you're going to watch it."

"We will if we can!" Leona said.

Holly chimed in. "Your band sounded great out there. I hope we can play together sometime."

"Yeah, that would be great," Sage said. She knew she was going to miss both girls. But she was also super excited to return to Starland and get back to the academy to show Lady Stella all the wish energy the Star Darlings had collected. And to share how she had figured out the key to changing the bad wish into a good one. Sage was ambitious and eager to prove her worth.

Scarlet turned to the Star Darlings. "Wait, before we go, I've got to do something."

Sage tried to stop her as she walked off. She called out, "Scarlet! We need to leave. . . ."

Scarlet assured Sage, "I'll be right back!

Promise!" She rushed from backstage into the theater and looked around, but it had mostly emptied out. Then she headed out the main arts center entrance. She was so absorbed in her feelings she didn't notice that it had started to rain lightly as she ran outside in search of Maxwell. She knew he had been at the show to see his sister perform, so he couldn't have gone far. She ran toward Port Harbor, where she and Maxwell had first taken a walk and gotten to know each other. Tears ran down her face. She had to say good-bye to the Wishling boy who had stolen her heart. She knew that she would probably never see him again.

She spotted him with his skateboard, walking toward the skate park.

She took a deep breath and caught up with him. "I'm leaving now." Swept up in the moment, she took her lucky fuchsia drumsticks out of her back pocket and handed them to Maxwell. She whispered, "To remember me by."

Maxwell didn't understand. "What? Where are you going?"

Scarlet got choked up. She held back her tears. "Home," she said.

"But I thought you lived around here."

She hesitated. "There's a lot to explain. I just can't right now."

He reached out to hug her, and she let him. Even though they were standing out in the rain, soaking wet, Scarlet wished they could stay like that forever, but she knew that she was a Starling and he was a Wishling, and as much as she could dream about it, their worlds would never fit together.

Scarlet erased Maxwell's memory of her and everything that had transpired between them. She quickly ran back toward the theater to find the other Star Darlings and return to Starland. She never looked back.

The rain had stopped. Maxwell shook himself out of what felt like a dream. He looked down and discovered a pair of hot-pink drumsticks in his hand.

A warm feeling shot through his body when he touched them. He smiled, but he had no memory of Scarlet or what had happened between them. He put the sticks in his backpack, put on his headphones, and started to listen to his new favorite song, "Far Away." He jumped on his skateboard and took off.

CHAPTER
Nineteen

The Time of New Beginnings had officially arrived in Starland by the time the Star Darlings returned. The featherjabbers and druderwomps were in full bloom. Preparation for Light Giving Day had started. The Celestial Café sizzled with excitement. Steaming moonberry crumble cooled on trays while bluebeezle beam puffs chilled in the kitchen's cosmic freezers. Sparkling energy filled the bright sky. The soothing sweet, fruity fragrance in the air reminded all the Starlings that a celebration was about to take place. Thanks to the Star Darlings' successful Wish Mission,

Starland glowed extra brightly on that glorious day.

Below the bustling campus, in the labyrinth of the underground caves, Lady Stella met with the returning Star Darlings in the Wish Cavern. The other seven Star Darlings were there, too, to honor their friends, who were back safe from Wishworld.

Sage, Libby, Leona, Vega, and Scarlet stood in front of Lady Stella, ready to receive their accolades for their stellar Wish Mission. Lady Stella began to speak. "My Star Darlings, may I commend you on succeeding in this most difficult Wish Mission. You showed us what true Star Darlings you were when you discovered the best part of yourselves to overcome a Wishling's misguided wish, and you even helped one of our own Starlings, Vivica, to see the best part of herself."

The girls smiled at each other.

Lady Stella continued, "Above all, you may not have gotten Rancora's teardrop pendant, but you did something more important—you made a very important discovery. One I hadn't even known about myself or figured out in all my years of wish granting. You figured out that when the right music is played at the right time, for the right person, it can change hearts and minds. Music has the power to inspire immense positivity."

She acknowledged Sage. "Your leadership during the mission did not go unnoticed. I see greatness in you, Sage."

Sage glowed, overcome with the feeling of accomplishment, having helped her home star. She looked forward to more Wish Missions for Starland. She bowed her head at Lady Stella. "Celestial gratitude," she said, beaming a warm lavender glow.

Each of the five returning Star Darlings was given a new Wish Blossom. Sage's boheminella blossom glowed with a soothing lavender light. Scarlet's dark and mysterious punkypow flower emanated a vibrant radiance, and Leona's golden roar bloom shined brightly. Libby's blushbelle, with its puffs of sparkling stardust, and Vega's richly colored bluebubble practically lit up the entire room. The blossoms, along with their

Power Crystals, warmed the cave with a healing light.

"Before the Light Giving Day's celebration commences, I want to share with you that after much contemplation, I have made the decision to allow Vivica to stay here among us at Starling Academy."

The Star Darlings were surprised that after Vivica had betrayed Lady Stella and Starland, Lady Stella would even consider forgiving her for what she had done.

Lady Stella explained, "Vivica was under the influence of a powerful amount of negative energy. She is a talented Starling and in many ways has earned her place here at Starling Academy. I will keep a close eye on her during a short probationary period. I'd like you to consider the matter closed." She paused, thinking about all that the five Star Darlings had overcome. "I ask you, Star Darlings, to give Vivica a second chance. I did, and I expect the same of you."

She looked into each of the five pairs of Star Darlings eyes that had faced Vivica and witnessed her dark side. "I understand your concern, but we're safe now. Thanks to you, Starland has the positive wish energy it needs to thrive. Of course, there will be more good wishes to grant, but for now, until a Wish Orb becomes active again and the timing is right for a good wish to be granted, we must celebrate our victory over Rancora and the great success of your mission." She smiled. "Speaking of celebrations, it's Light Giving Day. Shall we join the others?"

Lady Stella led the Star Darlings up the winding stairs into the open air to enjoy the festivities. She watched as the Star Darlings carefully dispersed, so as not to call attention to themselves.

A bright, colorful sunburst display filled the sky and a solar-horn resounded, signaling the start of the celebration. "Time to rejoice!" said Lady Stella.

The Light Giving Day celebration was in full swing. All the students at Starling Academy participated in the wondrous day of stargazing and gift giving. Some Starlings danced under the starry sky barefoot, while others snacked on cocomoons and ozziefruit cake. Bot-Bots buzzed around with serving trays of moonberry crumble and bluebeezle beam puffs.

As the Starlings picnicked and exchanged glowing gifts with one another, MO-J4 circled around Sage, who sat with Leona. He spoke excitedly. "Nice to have you back, Miss Sage." He had missed his favorite Starling. "Starland hasn't been the same without you."

Sage giggled under the glow of the luminous sky. "So happy to be back home, Mojay!" She reached behind her back and presented him with a gift.

"For me?"

"Yes." Sage smiled. "Open it!"

MO-J4 quickly unwrapped the gift. It was a recording of "When We Shine," the song the Star Darlings had written on Wishworld. "I look forward to listening to your musical creation." He bleeped. "I must attend to the other Star Darlings now." He zoomed off, carefully storing the recording in his star processing drive.

Leona had a gift for her roommate. "I don't see Scarlet anywhere," she said.

Scarlet sat on a hill high above the festivities, off by herself, under a glorange blossom tree. Leona Star-Zapped her: WHERE ARE YOU? I HAVE A PRESENT FOR YOU AND WE'RE GOING TO PLAY OUR SONG SOON!

I'LL BE THERE IN A STARMIN, Scarlet quickly Star-Zapped back. She needed some time away from the rest of the Starlings. She still couldn't shake her thoughts of Maxwell from her mind. It would be the first time the Star Darlings band would play "When We Shine" on Starland, and she knew it would bring back her memories of her time on Wishworld and of Maxwell. She reflected on her short stay in Port Harbor, where so much had transpired, and where she had opened her heart for the first time. She knew that there was nothing she could do right then but play the song with the Star Darlings. She reached for the lucky drumsticks that were always in her back pocket, but they were gone! Then she remembered where they were: on Wishworld! "Starf!" she exclaimed. Caught up in the emotion of the moment when she had said good-bye to Maxwell, Scarlet had given him her drumsticks to remember her by, something expressly forbidden on Starland!

c⟋⟍

Down in the band shell, Leona set up the microphone. "Where is Scarlet?" she asked Sage.

Sage pointed into the audience of Starling Academy students that was slowly gathering. "There she is!"

Out of breath, Scarlet hurried onto the stage. Leona rushed over to her. "Before we play, I wanted to give you a gift for Light Giving Day, roomie."

Scarlet didn't have time for a gift. She needed to figure out how she would play the song without her lucky sticks. "I can't right now."

Leona insisted, "Scarlet, open it!"

"Okay, okay." Scarlet hurriedly opened the gift and looked down at it. Her mouth formed a reluctant smile. Leona had given Scarlet a set of sparkling pink drumsticks! They were similar to her old ones but with a cool new pattern. Leona couldn't imagine how much this gift meant to her. "They're perfect. Thank you," Scarlet told her.

Leona asked, "Are you getting emotional on me, Scarlet? I didn't know a new set of drumsticks would have such an impact."

Scarlet tried to brush it off; she had to keep up her tough-girl reputation. "I'm all good. Thanks, Leona."

"So you like them, really?"

"You have no idea." Scarlet lifted the drumsticks from the box and held them like they were the last set on Starland.

It was time for the Star Darlings to perform. Sage checked that all the Star Darlings were tuned up and ready to play. She approached the microphone. "Hello, Starling Academy! Happy Light Giving Day! We're here to play you our new song. We hope you enjoy it. It's called 'When We Shine'!"

Vivica was there alone, standing apart from the other students. She watched the Star Darlings perform onstage, and some of the old feelings came back. She couldn't help feeling miserable:

there they were onstage, admired by the whole student body, while she was in the background, watching them soak up the starlight. She was just another student—and on probation at that. Vivica's whole body filled with anger. Her face tightened, and her aura turned gray, blue, and black. *Nothing has changed!* she realized. *I will always be in the shadows as long as the Star Darlings are the chosen ones.*

Later, Lady Stella was back at her office, about to shut down for the night and go back to her home at the top of StarProf Row, when she remembered a box the Bot-Bots had given her a few weeks earlier, after she'd had them remove and contain all the negative energy Rancora had been storing on the Isle of Misera. The box contained a few of Rancora's personal effects, mostly junk—things Lady Stella wasn't sure what to do with. She suddenly felt the urge to get rid of them. Something about the Time of New Beginnings always made her want to get rid of clutter and freshen up her space.

Lady Stella pulled the small box from the closet where she had kept it, and walked down the long flight of stairs to the fountain in the Wish Cavern below her office. Its water was charged with positivity, the perfect way to dispose of Rancora's belongings. First Lady Stella tossed in an old, ratty scarf, then a spell book titled *Negatite Magic*. There were some coins from Wishworld that Rancora had collected when she was there. She got rid of those, too. And there was a small metal tin, which Stella was about to toss but then felt compelled to open. Inside was a piece of paper, folded into a tiny square. Lady Stella recognized the page immediately, and her surprise caused her to lose her breath for a moment.

It was the page from the oracle Rancora had stolen.

As Lady Stella unfolded it, the words that appeared before her eyes made her glow turn completely pale.

A dark Starling will rise and determine the ultimate fate of Starland.

In that moment she understood why Rancora had sent Vivica on the Wish Mission. Vivica was the dark Starling, and Rancora was trying to control her. Lady Stella carefully slipped the piece of paper into her pocket and headed back up to her office to start making plans.

"This," she whispered to herself as she climbed the stairs, "this changes *everything*."